A RIDDLE OF ROSES

by

Caryl Cude Mullin

SECOND
STORY
Press

CANADIAN CATALOGUING IN PUBLICATION DATA

Mullin, Caryl Cude
A riddle of roses

ISBN 1-896764-28-2

I. Title.

PS8576.U433R52 2000   jC813'.6   C00-930169-0
PZ7.M9194Ri 2000

Edited by Catherine Marjoribanks
Cover art and illustrations by Kasia Charko

*Second Story Press gratefully acknowledges the assistance of the Ontario Arts
Council and the Canada Council for the Arts for our publishing program.
We acknowledge the financial support of the Government of Canada
through the Book Publishing Industry Development Program
(BPIDP) for our publishing activities.*

Printed and bound in Canada

Published by

SECOND STORY PRESS

*720 Bathurst Street, Suite 301
Toronto, Canada M5S 2R4*

To Stephen,
my companion in the quest

Acknowledgements

I gratefully thank Second Story Press for taking a risk and publishing the work of a completely unknown author. Special thanks to Catherine Marjoribanks, a gem amongst editors, and Beth McAuley for her support and encouragement at every step. Thank you to David McLauchlan, who was there from the very beginning offering advice and wise council. Many thanks to Roderick Cornell for providing me with such a flexible schedule at work. Thank you to Fiona Black, who cheered me on, and Pat Dearling, who gave me the occasional kick in the pants. Thanks to Reuben and Nick who inspired the songs and rhymes. The greatest thanks of all to my parents, Wilf and Mary-Pat, for first teaching me to love stories.

CHAPTER ONE

MERYL LEANED BACK on her heels, brushing her long, unruly red hair behind her ears with one hand and shoving the floor brush into a bucket of grizzled soapsuds with the other. The small stone cottage was impeccably tidy, and the late-afternoon sunshine made the newly scrubbed flagstones gleam like polished agate. She began jabbing at the few remaining bubbles, a frown on her face. Finally she gave an exasperated sigh and dropped the brush back into the water, which sent dirty flecks flying across the floor's freshly cleaned surface.

"Who cares," she grumbled. "Derwena won't notice anyway."

She lifted the bucket by the worn wooden handle and carried it out into the yard, where she promptly dumped it over a patch of crotchety marigolds.

The courtyard was warm and peacefully drowsy, but Meryl found none of the contentment there that she should have after a hard day's work.

"It isn't fair," she grumbled to a nearby hawthorn bush. "Why am I wasting my time with house chores? I should be living at the Hall with the other apprentices, learning my craft! No one gets to be a bard by chopping wood or scrubbing floors. People come from all over the island of Albaine — even from lands beyond — to learn from the Masters of the Hall. And here I am, a stone's throw away, and what am I doing? Watering flowers." She snorted in disgust and her amber eyes flashed angrily. After all, she was a mabinog, a bard in training, and she had better things to be doing!

Knowing that this year-long exile from the Hall was her own fault didn't make it any easier. After the last Samhain festival, when autumn had reddened the leaves and the first chill of winter had touched the air, heralding in the new year, Meryl had crept into the Scriptorium and secretly read the most hallowed of books: the great bard Taliesin's collection of songs and adventures.

Even now, as she raged over her punishment, the memory of those stories thrilled her. She shivered in the sunshine recalling Taliesin's tale of his first taste of the brew in a magic cauldron and his desperate flight from the enchantress who guarded it. He had been only thirteen, Meryl's age, and his swallowing of those three magical drops had instantly transformed him into the greatest bard the world had ever known. From that moment on, his life had been filled with one breathtaking adventure after another. He'd served King Arthur as poet and prophet, and he'd gone on long journeys in the company of fairies. He wrote about his conversations with the ancient gods of Albaine as easily as Meryl talked about playing tag with her friends. He'd been a student and friend of Merlin the magician. He claimed to have been to the legendary island of Avalon, the most sacred spot in the land. His life was nothing like her dull existence at the Hall, where becoming a bard meant years of study, full of endless memorization of songs and stories that everybody already knew.

Meryl knew that only the Masters were permitted to read the book, but she'd been unable to resist the temptation to look at those pages herself, to feel closer to the great bard of legend, to imagine herself journeying afar and coming back to the Hall with newfound wisdom to share. Taliesin had never followed the rules when it suited him to do otherwise, and the Masters of the Hall always praised him for his fearless character. She just couldn't see how it would hurt anyone if she took a little peek at his book herself, so that she could dream of what she, too, might someday know.

Her offense had been grave in the eyes of the Council. Anyone else would have been expelled from the Hall immediately for such disobedience. But Meryl's mother, herself Chief Bard, had died suddenly that summer, so Meryl's crime was seen as an act of rebellious grief. She was suspended from attendance at the Hall, and from all her studies, for one year. She was allowed no contact with anyone — bard, mabinog or servant — and would not be readmitted until the next Samhain festival, *if* the Council of Bards saw that she had learned her lesson. Now she lived with Derwena, the Mistress of Woodcraft, in a small cottage apart from the Hall itself, serving her as a common drudge.

Meryl glared at the marigolds. She had raised them from seeds herself over the course of the long winter of her exile and had planted them outside at Beltaine, in honour of the spring festival. She had hoped that if she could show Derwena how gifted she was in woodcraft, the Mistress might waver and tutor her in the ancient skills. It wasn't what she wanted most to learn, but at least she wouldn't feel as though her time was being wasted completely. Nevertheless, the Mistress simply watched her efforts with sympathetic eyes and gave her more tedious chores to do. The sentence of suspension had seemed a blessing when she had feared expulsion, but now the dreary months of mindless work were taking their toll.

"Why don't you just go ahead and die?" she snapped at the marigolds. "If you can't help me, then I won't have anything more to do with you." She stomped across the courtyard and flung herself on a stone bench that nestled against an ancient, crumbling wall.

That's where Derwena found her an hour later, glowering at the world. Meryl didn't even bother to look up at the sound of the Mistress's footsteps. The Woodcrone pursed her lips and shook her head regretfully. "Supper needs to be made," she said gently. Meryl's scowl deepened. With a sigh the Woodcrone hobbled over to the bench and sat down beside the girl.

To Meryl, the Mistress seemed to be as ancient as the Hall itself, resembling one of the sacred, wizened apple trees she tended. Her hair snaked down her stooped back in one thick, snowy braid, but her dark eyes still gleamed, penetratingly bright, from their nest of wrinkled skin. Meryl knew that she suffered from rheumatism, yet her aches never kept her from her teaching duties. Traditionally, bards served as healers as well as storytellers to the communities they traveled to, so every year Derwena led the older mabinogs through fields and woods, showing them the plants and herbs a bard was expected to recognize and know the purposes for.

After enduring the girl's sullen silence for a moment, the Mistress said, "Punishment is never easy. That does not mean it isn't good."

Meryl broke off a sprig from a rosebush beside her, grunting in annoyance. She ignored Derwena's raised eyebrows, a comment on the destructive act. The mabinog began to swish the sprig about her feet like a whip; then she tossed it down, jumped up and ground it with her heel. She turned on the Mistress.

"Punishment? This is torture, not punishment! A year in exile for reading a book — hasn't the Council's wounded pride healed yet?!" She stamped her foot again, already regretting her words and yet unable to stop them. It didn't help that Derwena just looked at her calmly; it made her own passion all the more humiliating.

"The sentence was just, as you well know," the Mistress replied sternly. "It is not simply a matter of a book and wounded pride. It is a matter of obedience. All bards must know how to obey if they wish to serve Art with any integrity. That is your lesson, and I suggest that you begin to learn it. You may start by preparing potatoes for our supper." She leaned down and picked up the crushed rose sprig, cradling it in her gnarled old hands.

Meryl was ashamed, but she was also determined. Over the past week, she had been devising a plan of escape, and she gave voice to it now.

"I can't stand it, Mistress. I wish that I could, but it's impossible. I want to leave. It's too hard being so close to the Hall yet completely separated from it. I haven't talked to Finian in months, and he's my best friend! We helped each other with our memorization, and cheered each other up when he got homesick for Eire, or I got lonely for my mother ..." Here Meryl choked on her words, but she shook her head and continued. She would honour her mother's strength with strength of her own, not with tears. "I want to be near the Great Hearth once again. I miss learning new stories, and I'm afraid I'll forget everything I've learned — no one has tested me on my triads since my suspension. I even miss Scripting class!" Her voice broke again, but she steadied it and went on. "If I can't be a part of the Hall, then I don't want to be near the Hall. I want to go away." Meryl looked at the Mistress pleadingly.

"My child, it is not for you to set the terms of your punishment. It was fashioned so that it would weigh heavily upon your spirit in just this way. If you leave, then you break the terms of your agreement with the Hall. It will be seen as another act of disobedience. You will not be permitted to return. Ever." There was no mistaking the note of finality in the Mistress's voice. Then her look softened, and she put an arm around the girl's shoulders. "There is only a little time left to your suspension, though it seems long now. Your friend Finian misses you, too, and looks forward to your return. Surely you can learn patience, child, and not do anything to jeopardize your calling. I know, as all do, how much being a bard means to you."

Meryl fought against her waning hope. "But there is another way, perhaps." She rushed on before Derwena could interrupt. "Taliesin wrote about people who were deemed bards after they had fulfilled some sort of quest. I thought that if I went on a quest for something and came back successful, then I'd have to be allowed back into the Hall. I'd have shown them that I'm worthy of the title. Don't you think they'd have to accept me then?"

Derwena smiled fondly at her young charge and thought carefully before answering.

"It used to be that following the Art was a true calling, and a dangerous one. A bard had to make her way in the world, travelling in search of truth with no home to shelter her, often with no friends to rely on, prey to whatever evils she might discover. Yes, there was a time when bards were made by deeds, not studies. As a result there were fewer of them," Derwena added dryly. "But as time passed, it came to be seen as an irresponsible waste of talent to send gifted people out into the world in this manner. That's why, centuries ago, the Hall was founded: to provide bards with a haven so that they might learn from the Masters, a safe place where they could develop and practise their skills before taking them into the world." Pensively the old woman stroked the damaged rose sprig. When she finally spoke again, Meryl wondered if the Mistress was growing senile; what she said didn't seem to have any connection to what they'd just been talking about.

"So many songs and poems have been written about this flower. Too many to count. Taliesin himself loved it greatly. This was his bush, you know." Meryl's jaw dropped. "Wonderful, isn't it? Few know it, but he planted it and tended it all his life."

Meryl took the sprig from the Mistress gingerly. The great bard's rose! And she had stepped on it in a temper. She blushed at the memory.

"It's also said," Derwena continued, "that the only time he'd pluck a bloom was when he was leaving on a new quest. The flower was a reminder of home, and a symbol for a safe journey. On his return, the first thing he'd do was bury the rose at the foot of this bush." Her eyes rested on the sprig in Meryl's hands. "It is not so beautiful as a bloom, perhaps, but I think it will do as a symbol for your own journey." She smiled at Meryl's astonished expression. "Perhaps it's a better symbol for you, anyway. You have not yet bloomed either."

"So I may go? And, if I do well, I may come back?" Meryl could hardly believe her ears.

Derwena sighed and looked about her. "The Hall is my home, child. I was trained here from childhood, much as you were yourself." The sounding of the evening chore bell interrupted them, and Derwena paused to listen. Meryl fought against her impatience; the Woodcrone had not answered her question.

Shaking her head free of the spell of the bell's tolling, the Mistress went on. "Many gifted students have been raised to Masters here, keeping alive the traditions of the Hall. And yet with each generation I see more Keepers, and fewer Makers, of Art. The Hall is changing, small one. I do not know if you will welcome it as home when you do return."

"So you're saying that I have to choose, aren't you?" Meryl said bitterly. "I either stay and rot in suspension, or I leave and never have the right to return. It doesn't sound like much of a choice to me."

"Oh, there is a choice, child, but the options are not as you see them. If you stay you will become a Master one day, for you have great ability." The Mistress stared shrewdly at Meryl. "But

I do not think that a life of copying texts, or caring for a herb patch, or telling the same stories to the same group of people year after year would grant you much pleasure."

Meryl didn't know what to say. Life at the Hall was often tedious for a mabinog, she knew that. Would a Master's life also be so dull?

"If you have the quest fire in you, why, then you must tread another path altogether. You must wander wherever you are led and find the truths that wait for you there, the knowledge that is meant for you alone to discover. Use your gifts, child, and sing these truths that we all may hear them. That is what a bard must do. Sing the songs, the stories of your travel, to whomever you may meet, and then bring them home again to us. You will learn along the way, enduring hardships beyond imagining. In the end you will be dead, or you will be broken, or you will be a bard. But you will not, I believe, ever be a Master of this Hall. That is your choice, my dear."

Meryl thought of the dangers of the quest and the safety of the Hall.

"I'll stay," she said.

Derwena made no response.

Then a vision of endless potato pots arose in Meryl's mind, along with memories of the Scripter, and of triads repeated over and over again on a hot summer's afternoon. She twirled the rose sprig between her fingers and thought again of Taliesin.

"I'll go."

Derwena still said nothing.

"I'll go, I'm going," Meryl said, firmly now. "And one day I'll come back a bard, Mistress. You'll see."

"I hope so, bright one," the Woodcrone replied.

CHAPTER TWO

MERYL WALKED INTO the shadows of the forest and stopped to take a deep breath, filling her lungs with the healthy pungency of growing things and dying things and the scent of animals. The Council had reluctantly agreed to her journey, and she had taken leave of the Hall only two days after making her decision. The day before she left, her friend Finian had crept to the cottage to say goodbye, and to warn her of the dangers he had heard of in the world beyond the Hall — of fairy folk and enchanted beasts and other fanciful legends that fired his imagination. Meryl reflected that he had always been a superstitious and excitable fellow. She hoped he would not get into trouble for missing a lesson.

Now she was truly alone. She had decided to avoid all roads for the time being. Her path was still unsure, and she didn't want to fall into the trap of going in whichever direction was most convenient. Besides, the solitude was comforting. She wasn't ready to face the curious questions of strangers yet.

The traders and travellers who came to the Hall sneered at those who moved through its sombre corridors and strolled about its yew- and oak-shadowed grounds. They said that the Masters were swollen with the idea that they were the Makers and Keepers of Art, an Art that they guarded jealously for themselves. But those same travellers fell silent when they passed the ancient grounds of the Hall, the heart of Albaine. The eerie snatches of song that flitted from the Masters and students working in the groves worked their enchantment upon even the most rational among them. They were always relieved to regain the open road and the world of clatter, commerce and good-natured bickering.

Awkwardly Meryl shifted the pack that she carried on her shoulders. It was heavier than she remembered it being, and she suspected that Derwena had added a few necessities. No doubt she'd be thankful for them later on, but the additional weight was an annoyance at the moment.

The forest grew increasingly dense as she moved beyond the domain of the Hall's guardian trees. Meryl began to stumble over roots, and she often had to stop to extract herself from the clutches of a bramble. She soon removed her heavy wool cloak and stuffed it into her already bulging sack. Her tunic and leggings gave her greater freedom of movement than her familiar mabinog's robe, but even so, walking was difficult. She was grateful for the tall leather boots that went up over her knees, for she fell often, barking her shins against stumps and fallen branches.

At the end of an hour, when she stumbled into a hidden sunlit glade, she collapsed on the grass as though she'd come to the end of a year's journey. Gazing up at the sky she muttered, "Derwena was right, I may be dead at the end of this. And right now," she added, grimacing as she felt her bruised shoulder, "that might be the most comfortable state to be in."

As she rested, she reflected on her last days at the Hall. It had not been easy to leave the only home she'd ever known. In a strange way, leaving the Hall had also meant leaving her mother; the two were joined in her mind.

With the thought of her mother she was suddenly caught up in the memory of a summer day, when she'd been only five years old. She had returned early to their shared room in the Hall to find her mother gazing out the window, wearing an expression of quiet rapture. Meryl had clambered up into her mother's lap and demanded, "Mother, what are you looking at?"

Her mother had laughed and hugged her tightly in her strong arms, arms that could play a harp for hours on end and still carry a tired daughter to bed. "I'm not looking," she replied. "I'm listening."

"To what?" the small Meryl demanded again, giving an impatient tug on one of her mother's thick, honey-coloured braids.

"To the land," her mother responded dreamily, gently extracting her hair from her daughter's grip.

"The land talks?" Meryl said, surprised. Her mother was always full of strange revelations. Even as a child Meryl had known that this made her special among all the bards.

"Of course," her mother replied. "It talks, it sings, it laughs, it weeps. It speaks to me, and I tell its story to the people."

Meryl listened intently. "All I hear is the cook scolding the kitchen boy," she said sourly. "I don't hear the land at all."

Her mother smiled and kissed the top of her head. "You will one day, small one," she said fondly. "The land recognizes you as one of its own. It told me so. Now, scamper! You have chores to do before supper."

The memory brought a familiar ache to Meryl's throat, but a sense of peace grew within her. She felt sure that her mother would have approved of her choice. The forest was ominous, even to one who had spent her life surrounded by trees. Yet Meryl felt secure in her mother's words: she belonged to the land. She let the quiet creep over her, and listened. Slowly she began to hear the gentle rustlings and whisperings of the trees, and it seemed that the world was singing her a lullaby.

Meryl shook off a drowsy afternoon-nap feeling and sat up. She decided to go through the contents of her sack to see exactly what she had in the way of supplies. Carefully she laid out the separate packages of biscuit, dried meat, medicinal herbs and the small purse of coins. Lying on the ground they seemed far less impressive then they had when she'd packed them. She really wasn't looking forward to eating that dried meat at all.

With a sigh she rifled through her sack again and frowned at the awkward, lumpy package she found at the bottom. Was it a gift from Derwena? She unwound it carefully, her hands beginning to tremble as it dawned on her what she held. A harp. Gently she rested it in the crook of her arm and brushed her fingers across the strings. Its tone was clear and pure, like a spring brook or a young child's laughter. The design of the instrument was delicate; its wooden frame was carved with interlacing knots and swirling patterns of leaves and birds. But though it looked fragile, it felt sturdy against her arm. A letter fluttered among the wrapping cloths and caught her eye. Meryl carefully set the harp down and picked up the short note.

"Child," it read, "this is a rare gift I give you, and not one I parted with easily. Yet I think a questing bard has more use for the harp of Taliesin than an old woman whose hands are too gnarled to make it ring true. Treasure it, small one, and it will honour you. Remember all that you have learned. Farewell."

Once again Meryl lifted the instrument: the harp of Taliesin. She could hardly believe her good fortune, or Derwena's generosity! She hoped that the Mistress would not be punished for the gift. Meryl didn't imagine that the Hall would relinquish such a treasure readily. Had the Council even known that Derwena had it in her possession? The idea of Derwena hiding the harp made her uncomfortable; she pushed the thought away. Derwena was indeed a woman of mysterious ways.

"Well, you're my harp now," she said aloud, in as firm a tone as she could muster. She began plucking at the strings, making sense of the harmonics. It was a frustrating task. As a mabinog she had had only minimal training in playing. Most of her time had been spent memorizing the triads, the verses that summarized legends and songs in three lines, which formed the basis of all storytelling.

"Well, now I know that the stories of you being a magical harp that can play on its own aren't true," she told the instrument ruefully, gazing down at her sore fingertips. She vowed to spend some time every day practising. The discipline would be good for her, and the skill would help her earn her living while she travelled. That small purse of coins could not be depended upon for long.

As she rewrapped the harp she came across the crushed rose sprig. Idly she turned it in her hands. "I'd like to just throw you away," she said to the plant, "but I guess Derwena's right, you are the perfect totem for my quest. Besides, you'll also remind me not to lose my temper. I promise to bring you home again." With that she wrapped the sprig in a bit of cloth torn from the harp's wrapping and placed it in the coin purse she had attached to her belt.

Next she ate some of the biscuit and chewed on a piece of the dried meat while she debated her course of action. She couldn't just blunder about the forest aimlessly, hoping that the direction of her quest would simply appear. She had to set herself a goal.

Morosely she regarded an ancient oak that stood on the other side of the clearing.

"Well, what do you think?" she said aloud. "Taliesin was captured by pirates and flung about on stormy seas until he washed up in a fishing weir. Amairgen had to journey to a new land, and was given the unpopular task of choosing which of his brothers would be king. It seems that most of the great bards had some contact with the ocean in the course of their journeys."

Meryl frowned, and began to carefully repack her belongings. The ocean sounded exciting, but terrifying as well. She knew too many stories in which the heroes either drowned or battled horrible monsters that lived in the deeps. The Hall did not think it necessary that its mabinogs know how to swim, let alone combat watery beasts. Meryl rubbed her nose in perplexity and then addressed the oak once more.

"Perhaps I must go to the ocean eventually, but I think I'll head north first. I'd like to put off my doom for as long as possible. Besides," she added cheerfully, "I've heard there are fewer people living up there, so there's less chance of me making an idiot of myself in front of a large crowd."

Meryl tied up her sack, adjusted her belt and faced north. She felt very solemn, and slightly ridiculous. "Goodbye," she said to the oak. Then she trudged back into the forest.

One day disappeared into the next, until finally a routine was established. Meryl slept no more than six hours each night. Her only other rests were for meals or practice sessions on the harp. At all other times she walked steadily north. Her muscles hardened, and she began to cover greater distances with each march. She learned how to walk silently through the woods, stepping with the toe of her foot first, rather then the heel. She learned how to smell for fresh water and filled her flask frequently at hidden springs. She recognized the different droppings of animals and could spot their paths, and so she knew when she was in danger of being caught on a hunting ground. She'd had some basic training in herb lore from Derwena, so she could gather familiar plants for food. From observation of the forest creatures she learned about others that were edible and many that were to be avoided.

The weather was wonderfully co-operative. Spring melted into early summer. Days and nights were warm, and the few times it rained, Meryl found comfort in her warm cloak beneath the sheltering trees. The forest welcomed her, and she called it home.

One warm, early-summer morning, Meryl heard the toll of a village bell ringing through the trees. She chewed through her last piece of dried meat and stared down her moment of decision. She could easily continue on in the forest, surviving as the creatures did on plants and mushrooms and small fish caught in forest streams, but she couldn't help seeing the end of her supplies as a sign. If she was going to be a bard she could hardly wander through the forest forever. She had gained some simple skill with the harp; not enough to be called a musician, but enough to accompany her singing.

"It's only a small village," she said to herself. "It's a chance to sleep in a real bed and eat some hot food. I can offer to sing for my supper at the local inn. If they say no, I can pay or leave, depending on how I feel. If they say yes, then I'll have my first real performance. There's nothing to lose."

She hoisted her pack onto her shoulder and began walking towards the village, intent on her mission. She didn't want to give herself the opportunity to back away from her plan.

CHAPTER THREE

MERYL SAT IN THE CORNER of the inn's common room, peering through the flickering, smoky light cast by thick tallow candles placed in sconces on all the walls. It was a warm, cheerful place, but Meryl, perched upon the high stool they had given her, felt as though she were being slowly stifled. Her throat tightened and her stomach twisted as she surveyed the crowd. It looked as though the entire village and its surrounding population had come out to hear her sing for her evening meal!

There was some shuffling among the people who were watching her. Faces swam in and out of focus. She noticed a farmer, chewing on a stalk of grain and looking at her as frankly and impassively as one of his cows. A woman with a pointy nose and chin watched her with a curious gaze that never wavered, all the while whispering earnestly to her equally fascinated companion. Meryl looked away, embarrassed, and her eyes met those of a young child, no more than four years of age, who had a dirty face and stared at her boldly with his fist shoved in his mouth. Meryl smiled at him, hoping to draw out a friendlier expression. He continued to stare unblinkingly for a moment, then withdrew his hand and stuck out his tongue.

Meryl fought back the panic rising in her throat. This was nothing like the performance classes she'd had at the Hall, where her only judges had been the classmates and teachers she'd known all her life. These faces were unfamiliar and cared nothing for her success or failure; either would be fine, as long as a show was provided.

Grimly she thought back over the events of the day. The landlord had been delighted with her request. Right away he'd sent runners all over the village to let people know that a minstrel had arrived at the inn and was going to perform that evening. Meryl was dismayed by the attention. She had hoped for a quiet, intimate performance with a bowl of hot soup at the end of it. Now she knew better what it meant to come as a stranger to a remote village. Likely all the villagers would have shown up, regardless of any announcement, just to watch her eat. She had simply made it easier for them to come and stare at her.

Angrily she pushed these thoughts away and concentrated on the tuning of her harp. Her hands were shaking, but she forced them to do the job required. When she was finished she looked up, summoning what she hoped was a copy of Rhydian's expression when he'd spoken at the Feast of Samhain. She had decided to begin with "The Most Tragic Tale of the Drowned Maiden." It was one of Rhydian's favourites; she'd seen him perform it a dozen times at least. It seemed like a safe choice; all the Masters insisted that it was an artistic gem. Meryl had always found it a bit drippy, but everyone else claimed to enjoy it.

She summoned all her courage and brushed her fingers across the harp strings in what was supposed to be a dramatic opening gesture. It probably would have been, had her index finger not gotten snagged. She had to wrench it free with a horrendous *twang*, which she immediately tried to cover up with the opening lines of the poem. Unfortunately, she was so unsettled by the harp that she began completely off-key and ended up bellowing discordantly the lines that Rhydian had said must always be sung quietly, with an air of mystery.

She struggled to correct her mistakes, but by the time the maiden in the song had looked out from her tower, "With a soulful sigh and a baleful stare," Meryl was ready to drown herself right along with her heroine. Her throat grew tight and dry, her tongue heavy and swollen, and still she rasped out the lyrics, thumping away at the famed harp of Taliesin with deadening regularity. She prayed that it would all be over soon.

The first snickers began at the back of the room. Meryl tried to ignore them, telling herself that it was likely only a few drunken brutes with no artistic sensibility. Her intonation grew even more tragic as she tried to sing over the interruption. The result was disastrous. The snickers turned into rumblings, and poured over the entire audience. Soon the whole room was shaking with laughter.

Meryl let her harp drop into her lap and stared in horror at the sea of derisive faces before her. Some boys in a group began to hiss and boo. An egg came sailing in on her left side and landed with a sickening splash at her feet. She covered her harp protectively with her arms and huddled upon her stool, a spectacle of shame.

The heckling grew louder. Another egg flew past her right ear. "They brought eggs?" was her only clear thought. "Were they planning to do this?" She felt very bitter indeed.

A huge figure loomed by her side, and Meryl choked back a scream. He was hairy and dirty, and his eyebrows had a singed appearance. He looked like a troll. Meryl wondered briefly if she'd have time to faint before he killed her.

Then a miracle occurred. The troll turned to the crowd and bellowed "Be ye quiet!"— and the crowd obeyed. He glanced at Meryl to see whether she was still breathing; she gave a hesitant smile to reassure him. Satisfied, he turned back to the room.

"And what will be the goings-on here, then? Do we ask a guest to sing, only to make her feel lowly by obligin' us?" His voice was surprisingly deep and pleasant.

A voice from the back answered him, "Sing, aye, but my grandmother croaks a fairer tune than that one there, Darren." This was greeted with a few half-hearted chuckles, but they quickly died out. Darren was apparently a force to be reckoned with.

"Well, Llew, it's no great story that a tune should jangle those tin pots ye've got hangin' about your head for ears, but I'm of a mind that the girl should not suffer for that. Come now, girl," he said, turning back to Meryl and looking at her in a kind way. "Sing us a tune, then — perhaps somethin' a bit more fittin' to the season. Winter's the time for moanin'. Let's have a glad song."

His request was not as simple as it seemed. More than anything she wanted to run into the woods and put her disgrace behind her, and this fellow was asking her to be merry. The Hall had never approved of humour as an Art form; she had never been taught any comic pieces. Her mind flipped desperately about, finding nothing to help her. Finally her fingers that came to her rescue. They had begun plucking out the tune of a song she had written to amuse the kitchen staff of the Hall. It was about one of the scullery boys and his tragic love for a goose whose life was cut short by the jealousy-maddened cook. She launched into the song with as much verve as she could muster. She could hardly do any worse, after all.

> Oh, goosey darling, lay nearby
> A golden egg, a love-lorn sigh,
> That on it I may gaze and dream
> Of heaven in a sauce of cream.

So it went, at times with more wit, usually with more folly. But it was the sort of joke that was often bandied about the village, and it was greeted with happy chuckles of approval. When it was done, honest applause, spattered though it was, met Meryl's ears. It did not erase the earlier humiliation, but it loosened the cruel fist of shame clenched in the pit of her stomach.

Her hero, for so she thought of Darren, called out, "There now, that was fair pleasin'. Sing us another then, will ye?"

She sang a song she'd written for Finian, a mock tragedy on the death of one of the Hall's Masters from the bite of a rabid squirrel. Meryl knew that she did a good job of imitating the Scripter's glare; she'd seen it often enough. And the villagers seemed to enjoy it greatly, judging from the way so many of them were leaning forward in their seats and tapping their feet to the chorus.

When she had finished, Meryl put down her harp, basking in the applause that followed. Now it was time for a story. She waited until a hush fell over the room, and then she began her tale. It was one of the stories that she'd read in Taliesin's book, about how the mighty King Bran had once journeyed to Eire to rescue his sister Branwen the Fair. The story itself was familiar, but Taliesin's version was gripping. Meryl told the story simply, without the sweeping gestures and dramatic intonation that she'd learned at the Hall, which had failed her so miserably earlier that evening. In the candlelight, her clear voice wove the story magically in the air.

When she had finished, her listeners sat quietly blinking, slowly coming out of the spell they'd been under. There was little applause, but Meryl didn't need it to know that she'd done well; the entranced faces surrounding her told her everything.

Gradually the people drifted away, murmuring both their thanks and their apologies. Darren was one of the last to make his departure. He came up to Meryl and said, "If ye'll stop by my smithy on the morrow, friend singer, I'll give ye some bread and some good strong cheese to send ye on your way."

Meryl looked up into his face. It was funny, she thought, how it now looked kind instead of frightening. "Thank you. I will come." She wanted to take his hand and tell him how grateful she was for what he'd done, but she felt too awkward. Instead she stared up at him and tried to keep from blushing. "Thank you for everything," she added, somewhat lamely.

"Aye, it was a tight spot ye were in. Even the best of folks is cranky when they're disappointed. There's no point in makin' someone a plough when all they need is a horseshoe, my father was always sayin', and I reckon ye've learned his meanin' tonight. Still, ye made a fair horseshoe once you got the way of it, and that's all that matters, I'm thinkin'. Well, peace go with ye," he said, suddenly looking uncomfortable. "I'll be off home."

The thought of her own simple bed at the Hall brought on a surge of homesickness. She bade him goodnight, fetched her hard-earned soup and bread from the cook and crept upstairs to her room. It took her a while to fall asleep, but when she did she slept the night through.

CHAPTER FOUR

MERYL ROSE WITH THE SUN and left the inn hastily. The embarrassment of "The Drowned Maiden" still haunted her, despite the fact that she had redeemed herself as a performer. She was sure that the memory of those eggs would be with her for the rest of her life. She debated whether she should seek out the smithy or not; part of her wanted to leave the village and put her humiliation as far behind her as possible. But she really did want to see Darren again. He had supported her, a total stranger, against the people he knew best. She owed him a proper farewell at the very least. Her stomach rumbled, and the memory of his offer of bread and cheese ended the debate.

The smithy was not difficult to find — Meryl simply followed the sound of clanging metal to a low stone building on the edge of the village, right beside the main road. It had three walls, while the front was protected from the elements by the long overhang of the sloping roof. This also sheltered a hitching post, where horses could stand in relative comfort while their hooves were seen to. The walls inside were blackened by years of smoke, yet the light and warmth of the hot smithy fire made the place cheerful.

Darren was merrily pounding out horseshoes. He was wearing a thick leather apron and heavy boots, yet his arms were bare, the sleeves of his linen shirt rolled up past his elbows. Meryl supposed he must be used to the heat radiating from the forge. She stood back and watched in awe as he turned the blistering metal into a perfect U with a few swift and precise strokes of the hammer. He plunged the horseshoe into the water bucket to cool it and then looked up at her with a grin. With a surprising gentleness of manner he put down his tools and extended his hand in greeting.

"There now, it's a grand thing to see another this early in the day. Come into the back and break your fast with me." He led her through the smoke and heat of the smithy to a small set of living quarters attached at the back.

Bread and cheese sounds like plain fare, but when the cheese is strong and ripe and the bread is warm and fresh, it's as fine a feast as queens or kings or bards alike could dream of. Meryl delighted in the meal, warming her toes at the hearth and her spirit in Darren's companionship. She felt so at ease with him that she chattered freely about her life at the Hall. She showed him the rose sprig she carried with her, like her hero Taliesin, and told him how she had come to be on this uncertain quest. He was a good listener.

She finished the last of her meal and sat back in her chair. Darren was looking at her thoughtfully; the sudden silence made her feel awkward. She was just about to make her farewells when he spoke.

"What I see here, then," he mused aloud, "is that ye've taken on to apprentice yourself — but ye've got no master. It's a hard path ye'll be followin', no mistake, and ye've only begun to travel it. Now listen here, friend." He leaned forward in his seat. "I don't know more than a blind cow about bardin', but I do know apprenticin'. And what I know is that if you're set on bein' a master of any trade, ye've got to start by bein' the servant. Ye start by learnin' the little things, and ye don't move on to the metal till ye've mastered the fire, so to speak."

Meryl interrupted him. "But Darren, I know this. The Masters at the Hall made me memorize triads and copy texts till I thought I'd bloat like a waterlogged toadstool. I've learned lots of the traditional songs and some of the most famous stories, and a little bit about how to perform in the accepted way. I've studied court etiquette and herb lore and even something of the laws that govern our land. I've followed in the Masters' footsteps and learned to honour the bards of old. I've done that part. Now I need to test my wings. That's why I left."

"Well now," he said pensively, "I'm not holdin' fault with the Hall. But it seems to me that the 'little things' I was referring to aren't those things ye just mentioned. Now take last night ..."

Meryl flushed scarlet — he was going to talk about that horrid "Drowned Maiden."

Darren saw her embarrassment, but he did not spare her from it. "Aye," he said seriously, "ye began poundin' on the iron when it was still in the stone last night. Now I'm sure it was a fine song ye tried to sing, but ye haven't smelted it and worked it and made it your own yet. It was just fancy words with no heart. Stick to the little rhymin' ye did. It may not be grand, but it's honest and true. There's no need for one who hasn't looked life in the face yet to be moanin' on about death. It only makes folks as are closer to it uncomfortable-like."

He grinned then, and thumped Meryl on the shoulder as he rose from his chair. "Well, horses don't shoe themselves, nor do songs fall from the sky, I'll be thinkin'. We've both of us a parcel of work to do, friend." He turned back into the smithy.

Meryl packed the food supplies he generously gave her, then followed after him. She wouldn't have to eat dried meat for a while, now.

Darren was at the fire, holding a small piece of iron in the flame with the tongs. It brightened until it seemed to be a small star hovering just beyond his reach. "I do love the way the hot metal goes dancin' with the hammer," he murmured. Then he flashed a delighted smile, asking, "Will ye sing us a song for the forgin', friend singer?"

It was impossible not to be affected by the joy that seemed to radiate from him, just as the heat did from the fire. Without a thought she began the "Stomping Song" she'd written one glorious, free day when she had gone hay-making. The threat of rain had caused a flurry of activity in bringing in the year's fodder harvest, and some of the junior mabinogs had been sent to lend a hand. Meryl had exulted in the rhythmic thumping necessary to press the loose hay down when it was thrown onto the cart, and the song had been born of that work. Everyone was singing it by the end of the day; it made the work pass quickly and seem like a festival.

Meryl had not sung the song since that day. She had come home to find her mother ill with the summer fever that a wanderer had brought to the Hall a week earlier. A tireless nurse, her mother had brought the stranger back to health and sent him on his way, only to find herself prey to the same sickness. Meryl had been separated from her to avoid further spread of the contagion. A few days later she had died.

Now Meryl sang her song with the memory of that pain still vivid. It lent an intensity to the song that had not been there in its original making. Darren took the small bar of metal from the flames and began to shape it with a tiny hammer that looked ridiculously delicate in his great paw. While Meryl sang, the metal appeared to mould itself to the character of the music, twisting and leaping in the tongs as though it really were dancing with the hammer. The song ended on a high note, just as Darren thrust his creation into the cooling bucket.

Meryl came closer to see what it was he had made. When she beheld it, she gasped. Darren had shaped a perfect iron rose, with both strength and fragile beauty.

"It's for ye, friend," Darren said shyly. "The thought came to me when ye spoke of the great Taliesin's rose. I thought ye'd be well off to have a rose of your own to keep ye company and to guide ye. I'll just be doin' a bit of finishin' work on it now, and then I'll fix it with a clasp such as fine ladies use to fasten on their jewellery."

As he continued to work on the brooch, Meryl again took the small, brittle rose sprig from her coin purse. She could throw it away now; Darren's rose was much finer. But she had promised to bring it home. It seemed silly to feel bound to a promise made to a dead plant, but Meryl put it back into her purse anyway.

When the iron rose was finally finished to Darren's satisfaction, Meryl took it gingerly into her hands. The metal was still a bit warm to the touch.

"It's lovely, Darren." Meryl traced the shape of the petals with her finger, marvelling at their intricacy. She suddenly felt as though she was going to cry. "I don't know how to thank you enough. You've rescued me, and fed me, and given me a beautiful gift, and all I've done for you is eat your food and talked your ear off. It's been a pretty poor exchange for you, I'm afraid."

Darren took the rose from her hand and fastened it onto her cloak. "I don't think I'm in agreement with ye there, now," he replied, looking into her eyes with a serious expression. "Ye gave me a fine song to be singin' while I'm workin' the metal, and I gave ye a bit o' the earth's pride to be wearin' while ye go about your travels. That's as fine a trade as was ever made between two Makers, I'm thinkin'. As for the rest of it, when friends sit and share there's no one keepin' a score to see who's givin' and who's receivin' the most. Those things can't be measured."

A farmer entered with a tool that needed repairing, so Meryl took her leave. Darren walked her to the door of the smithy.

"Fare ye well, friend," he said simply. "I hope ye travel through this way again. If ye do, know that ye've a place at my hearthside if ye wish it."

Meryl spluttered her thanks and hurried away, furious with herself for the tears welling up in her eyes. When she reached the border of the forest she looked back at the smoke rising from the forge and murmured, "Goodbye, friend smith." Then she dove back into the forest and marched resolutely north.

CHAPTER FIVE

For another week she travelled, still moving northward, bathed in the soft summer warmth of the forest. She practised on the harp, composed pleasant rambling songs, and invented marvellous adventures for herself to encounter. In her mind she met with kings and queens and enthralled them with her music, or encountered roving bands of gypsies whose awe and respect she won through her storytelling. She dreamed of knights falling at her feet in adoration, and magical doors to the otherworld being opened, ushering her into one brave deed after another.

By the end of the week, however, she had grown tired of her own company. On a day that was so hot even the forest shades shimmered, she sat down on a mossy couch beneath an oak and once again debated her future. Balling her cloak into a pillow, she rested against the tree and set her options before herself in logical order.

"Reasons for staying in the forest: I can practise at any time of the day or night and not disturb anyone; my lodging and my food are free; it's unlikely that I'll get waylaid by robbers; I don't have to travel with tedious companions. Reasons for leaving the forest and travelling by road: I can sleep in real beds; I don't have to find my food; I have the chance to improve my performance skills; I might get to talk to someone more responsive than this tree." Meryl paused and weighed the options in her mind, then came to a decision. "I can't be a bard without an audience. I must take the road."

"I wouldn't advise it, no how, no way."

Meryl leapt up, spun around — and saw no one. For a moment she wondered if the heat of the day had affected her mind.

"Pardon?" she queried.

"Hard of hearing, are you?" the voice answered sympathetically.

Meryl whirled in the direction it came from, but saw only a small bramble bush. Was she dealing with an invisible being?

"What I said was, I wouldn't advise going on the road," the voice went on conversationally. "They're generally nasty, dusty things crowded with people, *hruumph-nha*. You'd be much better off in the forest, indeed, indeed."

"I see," said Meryl, not seeing anything at all.

"Glad to be of help," replied the voice. "Actually," it went on, "I'm really very grateful indeed. It's been a while since anyone came to me for advice. I was beginning to wonder if I'd been forgotten entirely. Humans have such ridiculously short memories, *hruumph-nha*. I often think they'll just forget themselves out of existence, indeed I do. Well, goodbye," it finished abruptly.

It was such a thorough dismissal that Meryl very nearly picked up her sack and left. Then she caught herself — here was an adventure virtually sitting under her nose, and she was about to shake hands with it and leave. Neither Taliesin nor her mother would ever have let such an opportunity slip by. Straightening her back, she tried to strike a daring pose and demanded, "Please reveal yourself at once."

There was a moment of silence, then the voice muttered, "Well, I never," in shocked tones. This was followed by what sounded suspiciously like weeping.

"Marvellous, now I've gone and injured its feelings," Meryl thought. "It'll probably follow me and strangle me while I'm sleeping." The idea spurred her to apologize.

"Look, I'm sorry. I didn't mean to be rude. I'm just not used to talking to voices without bodies, that's all. Do you have one — a body, I mean?"

The weeping ceased immediately. "Of course I've a body, *hruumph-nha*. What sort of doltish question is that? If you've come all this way to be horrid and rude and stupid you can just toddle off and find some other draoi to bother. I think there's one in Eire who's accustomed to dealing with numskulls like yourself. No doubt the journey will do you good, indeed, indeed."

Meryl felt her mind flounder. "A what?" she asked.

"A *drow-ih*," the voice replied, speaking slowly and carefully, as one would to a child or a foreigner.

"A *drow-ih*," she repeated, equally carefully. "What's that?"

It was apparently the wrong question to ask — or the right one, depending on your point of view. It certainly brought about an immediate response. The bramble bush began to tremble, and the ground beneath it heaved and pitched, rising into a muddy heap of twigs and roots and dirt. The lump then sculpted itself before Meryl's startled eyes, becoming a person-shaped being moulded from the forest floor. Branches twisted into arms, roots into legs. Soil, moss and wood blended to form body and head, from which leaves sprouted in the manner of hair. It stood just over four feet tall when it had finally finished "growing," and the crown of its head was just level with Meryl's chin. It sneezed, blew a bit of gnarled wood Meryl took for its nose into a leaf, and glared up at the girl with a pair of glittering, brown-berry eyes that were strangely human in that alien face.

"I," the creature said pompously, "am a draoi."

Meryl felt her jaw hanging open and closed it with an effort. "I see," she said, lying for the second time that day. Awkwardly she bowed to the creature. "It is an honour to meet you, Master Draoi. My name is Meryl, and I am on a quest."

The draoi seemed pleased by the formal turn the conversation had taken. "Greetings, human," he replied. "I am Halstatt, the forest oracle." He gestured for Meryl to sit down, and then he followed suit with a great deal of snapping and groaning. "Ah," he said, once he was seated, his rooty legs stretched out in front of him, "that's much better, indeed, indeed. I haven't moved for a century or so, you see," he said confidentially to Meryl, "and one's limbs tend to get a bit brittle, *hruumph-nha*."

"Are you really an oracle?" Meryl asked excitedly. "I've heard about such things in stories. People would come from great distances to the special places where an oracle lived. They thought that gods spoke through the oracles, so they'd ask them all sorts of questions."

Meryl had been taught at the Hall that sometimes the oracle's answers were given through a priest or priestess, and sometimes they just came from a whispering sound in the trees. Sometimes the oracle would speak in riddles, so the questioner would have to puzzle out the answer herself. The oracles always spoke the truth, but it wasn't always easy to understand.

"Of course, the Masters at the Hall said all the stories were dreamed up by a few wise elders who had moved away from the community and become a bit odd —," she began again, but she realized she'd been speaking thoughtlessly when it became obvious that the draoi was in danger of having an apoplectic fit. He began to wring his hands and snap off his twig-like "fingers" in a most disconcerting manner.

"I suppose that it's all one can expect in these degenerate days, this ignorance. To think that I'd live to be brushed aside by a rabble of human storytellers. Well! It's enough to make an honest draoi burrow down and refuse to think, indeed, indeed. Why, the times were that every initiate bard had to make a pilgrimage to see me, not to mention all those dunderheaded lovers and warriors. Really, I don't know who was the most irritating. Now you listen to me," he said sternly. Meryl nodded; she didn't think she had much choice in the matter. "Much ridiculous nonsense has been told about we draoi by you humans over the years. You've probably had your head filled with tales of 'dryads' and other such rubbish, no doubt, no doubt indeed."

"Dryads!" said Meryl. "You mean tree spirits who haunt the woods and—"

Halstatt interrupted with a snort. "Yes, that's just the sort of twaddle I meant, *hruumph-nha*. You undoubtedly think that I spend my time cavorting about the glades with all my relatives, getting drunk on spoiled fruit juices and howling at the moon. Well, just forget all that. We draoi are a solitary, quiet race with no interest in gamboling about whatsoever, *hruumph-nha*. Yet, because we sit in one place and think things through properly, your people have made a tradition of coming to ask us for advice." He sniffed, somewhat arrogantly, Meryl thought.

"It's sheer laziness," the draoi added petulantly. "If you weren't so busy running about getting yourselves into trouble and actually sat down for a good long ponder you'd be so much better off. You'd probably live longer, too. Rootless, that's what you are; rootless. Really, it's incredible that you have any useful ideas at all, seeing how short-lived you are. Now I have been alive for exactly five hundred and eighty-nine years, as you humans record time, *hruumph-nha*." Halstatt broke off his tirade and looked down at his hands. If he'd been human, Meryl would have thought he looked shy.

"Actually, that's why I was so pleased to have a visitor today," he said, greatly subdued. "You see, it's my birthday."

"Many happy returns," said Meryl. She wondered how the draoi would have behaved if he hadn't been pleased to have a visitor.

"Well, now that you know what I am, how may I further assist you?" he asked pleasantly.

"Ah, pardon me?" Meryl asked.

Halstatt stood up, jumped up and down on the spot for a moment and then sat back down. He glared at Meryl. "Have we come all the way back to the beginning of this conversation? Am I going to have to explain everything to you one more time? Because if so, I warn you that I'm simply going to bury myself again and you can holler questions at me until you're blue in the face for all the good it will do you, indeed, indeed, indeed!"

Meryl stared at him blankly. "Do you want me to ask you a question?"

The draoi began to snap his fingers again. "Do I want you to ask me a question? Do *I* want you to ask me a question? Tempests and toadstools, I think the human is mad." He began to fling earth wildly about.

"Stop that!" she bellowed, wiping mud from her eye. "You're the one acting like a madman, not me!"

He stopped abruptly. "In point of fact," he said, in icy tones, "I would be acting like a mad-draoi, if you please, *hruumph-nha*. Now tell me plainly; did you, or did you not, say that you are on a quest?"

"I did. I mean, I am."

"Very well then. I am a draoi. I answer questions. I've already answered many of yours. If you are questing, then question." He folded his arms across his chest and glared at her.

Meryl blushed hotly. "Well, you needn't be so self-righteous about it. All you had to do was speak clearly in the first place and you might have avoided that last fit." She saw the warning signs of another with that comment, so she hurried on.

"I'm on a quest to learn how to be a bard, like mabinogs used to do in the old days before all our learning came from the

Hall. I suppose you could tell me how to go about doing that, if you wanted to."

"Oh, you suppose, do you? Indeed, indeed. Well, I suppose that it might be better for you to go questing for some manners, but then we draoi have never been able to teach you humans anything, *hruumph-nha*. Still, your question is straightforward. You must learn from the Masters. That is all." He began to dig again.

"What does that mean?" Meryl cried. "I can't go back to the Hall, I left so that I could learn the old way. Weren't you listening?" She felt like shaking him.

"Oh my roots and berries, is everything so complicated for you? There is no riddle here. I said the Masters, and I meant the Masters. I didn't say anything about that confounded Hall of yours, indeed, indeed I didn't. I've met some of its so-called bards before and I can't say I was impressed. There's more to the world than can be taught in your classrooms."

"But then who do you mean by the Masters?"

He turned to her and sniffed. "There you go, typical human, indeed, indeed, expecting a draoi to do all the thinking for you. You'll know a real Master well enough when you find one. Just keep your eyes open, if you see what I mean."

Meryl bit her tongue to keep from shrieking with frustration. Then another thought struck her, and from her cloak she pulled the flower Darren had made her. "A bit o' the earth's pride" he had called it. If anyone was a Master it was Darren. She had learned far more from him than she had in all her years at the Hall.

When she looked up she found Halstatt staring at the metal rose she held in her hand. "Isn't it beautiful?" she said, offering it to him so that he could see it better. "One of your 'Masters' made it for me."

He took it gently in his hands and turned it over for a

moment, then held it up to the sunlight. All at once he crumpled down into a twiggy heap and began to sob.

"For heaven's sake, what's the matter?" Meryl asked. She couldn't imagine what had upset him so.

"Lost, it's lost, forever, ever lost," he moaned.

Meryl leaned over him and began to thump his mossy back, saying, "There, there," as she had once seen the Hall's cook do to a weeping scullery boy. Halstatt ceased crying immediately and barked, "Stop that at once. What do you think I am, a belching child?" He returned the flower and sat up straight.

"I once had a rose, you see," he said, when he had regained his composure. "It was a magical rose that bloomed all year, even in the dead of winter. It used to burn like a flame in the snow. Magical things are rare nowadays. You humans tend to tromp all over them when you're too busy to look where you're going — which is most of the time, *hruumph-nha*."

Meryl was afraid that he'd forget his story and go off on another speech about human weaknesses, but the sight of her rose kept him on track.

"I tended my rose over the centuries and it bloomed in constant friendship. Then came the winter of the long snow. If you weren't such an absurdly short-lived creature you'd remember it as clearly as I do."

"I don't see how. I probably wasn't born yet," Meryl retorted.

Halstatt looked surprised and sputtered, "Hmm, indeed, indeed," before continuing.

"The woods were full of humans who wanted to know when spring would come, as if I were some sort of oracular groundhog, *hruumph-nha*. I was a bit tired of always being asked the same question, so I must confess that I was a bit gruff to anyone who came seeking advice. Well, there came a day that I was visited by one of your bard people —"

"Who?" demanded Meryl. It would be wonderful if she could discover a forgotten story.

"Taliesin, was his name."

"Taliesin!" Meryl shrieked. "Are you sure, Halstatt? Are you sure that was his name?"

"Of course I'm sure. I'm a draoi, I told you. We don't forget anything, especially the name of our greatest enemy, *hruumph-hruumph-nha.*"

Meryl's cheer died in her throat. "Enemy?" she responded weakly.

"Indeed, indeed. He came and sang and told me tales, and listened to all the wisest advice I had to give. He sang me to sleep, and when I woke he was gone. And my rose was gone with him." Halstatt snapped his jaw shut and glared at Meryl.

What could she think? Her greatest hero was a thief! The Hall would not like this story; she didn't like it herself. Taliesin loved roses, Derwena had said. With a flash her hand went to her purse and the dried rose sprig, but it fell away just as quickly. The sprig was from an ordinary bush. Meryl herself could vouch that it had never bloomed in winter. A magical rose would have been a tremendous temptation for Taliesin. He just might have taken it. But if he had ...?

"What did he do with the rose?" she mused aloud.

"If I knew that, do you think I'd be sitting here, *hruumph-nha?*" Halstatt barked.

Meryl stared at him in surprise. "Do you mean you can walk? Now, don't get angry," she said, noticing the warning signs of another fit. "I just didn't know, that's all."

"Of course I can walk," he snapped indignantly. "I'm a draoi, not a plant, you know."

"No, I didn't," she replied absent-mindedly. Her mind was back on the puzzle of Taliesin's theft. "He must have had a reason,

Halstatt. He was the greatest bard of all time. His songs brought light and hope into a dark age. After King Arthur was killed, it was Taliesin who carried his body to Avalon, bringing back the promise that one day the King would return to Albaine. It was Taliesin who encouraged the knights of the land to continue to fight for truth and justice. It was Taliesin who founded the school for bards that grew into the Hall. Everything he did was an effort to make the land and its people better and more noble. He would never take your treasure, at least not without a worthy reason. I'm sure of it."

"Well, I know the reason, indeed, indeed I do. It was greed, pure and simple, and there's your greatest bard for you." He began to splutter and snap again.

"No, I can't believe it," Meryl replied. "I'm going to find the reason, Halstatt. And I'm going to do more than that — I'm also going to find your rose."

Halstatt immediately jumped up out of his hole and busily began to fill it in. In a few moments the earth was flat and smooth; once the moss grew over it, no one would be able to guess that the ground had been disturbed.

"Right, then," he said, shambling over to stand beside her. "I'm ready to go."

"Go? Go where?"

"With you, of course. *Hruumph-nha*, you are simple-minded aren't you? Did you think I'd let you go off and find my rose without me?"

Meryl panicked. She was not at all sure that she wanted a travelling companion, let alone such a temperamental one as the draoi.

"But you hate moving around! You make fun of humans because they don't sit still like you do. If you come, who will do the thinking here?" she cried desperately.

"I can move and think at the same time, thank you very much, *hruumph-nha*. And you needn't worry about me slowing you down. I'm a young, adventurous draoi yet, indeed, indeed. Besides," he added helpfully, "it will aid your questing if you have a draoi to ask questions of all the time."

"But Halstatt, I don't even know where I'm going," Meryl replied as reasonably as she could. "I have no idea where to begin looking. I'll probably just blunder about the country until I find something, and you'll hate that."

"There! You do need me after all!" declared the draoi triumphantly.

"I don't see how," said Meryl.

"Of course you don't. But I do, indeed, indeed. While the wretch was staying with me he asked me many questions about the rose. I was only too happy to talk about my treasure, not knowing that I was nurturing a viper at my breast, *hruumph-nha*. He asked me where it came from, and I told him that it had belonged to my mother. She had brought it from the west when she came seeking a quiet place of her own. She told me that she had gotten it in a 'land of eternal summer.'"

"Avalon!" breathed Meryl rapturously.

"Yes, that's just what he said, and with the same greedy light in his eyes, I might add, indeed, indeed."

Meryl tried to look less excited, and failed. "Halstatt, that's in the magical otherworld, a fairy land ruled over by the Queen of the Winds. It's the fairies' most holy place. The stories say that it's always summer there, and that King Arthur sleeps in the Queen's castle with his sword, Excalibur, resting by his side. It's not supposed to be a real place you can travel to, or that's what they say at the Hall. It's filled with wonders. Why," she exclaimed, her eyes getting rounder, "the magic cauldron of Ceridwen is there. Anyone who sips from it becomes a true bard! Think of that, Halstatt. One drink and I'd be a bard, just like Taliesin, and no one at the Hall could question it." She felt herself growing giddy.

"*Hruumph-nha*, typical human. Rush in and get in a second something that should take years of work to develop. Foolish, foolish. However, it would seem that that's where the fiend would go. So, you see, you do need me. Magical places are human-shy, and an honest draoi is your best chance for admission. Agreed?"

It was hard to argue with a draoi. "All right," said Meryl.

"Good. First we go south, then we go west."

And so they went.

Chapter Six

Halstatt kept his promise. By the third day of their journey it was Meryl who was in danger of slowing down the draoi, rather than the reverse. He scuttled through the underbrush, an ambulatory bush rustling through the forest at a steady pace and never losing his footing. And the only thing swifter than Halstatt's stride, it seemed, was his tongue. It was as though he was determined to make up for a century of solitude with one steady stream of conversation. If Meryl wanted to practise, she had to slink away when they stopped to rest. If she didn't, Halstatt would critique every note she played and every word she sang. Leaving saved her sanity, and his life.

It was late afternoon on the fourth day of their journey when they came upon a cottage made of stacked logs with a thatched roof, clinging to the edge of a forest path. On either side of the door, a large, mullioned window, with many small panes of glass, flashed in the sunlight as though it were made of gemstones. And standing in the yard, greeting visitors, was a beautiful wooden statue of a young woman playing a harp. But what was most remarkable was the inordinate number of cats about the house. There were large orange tomcats sunning themselves on the flagstones, silver tabbies stalking invisible quarry, prowling black miniature panthers, sleek white duchesses, calico queens, and howling creatures of brown and grey that struck up a chorus when the pair of travellers came into view. Halstatt put his hands over his ears and began to whimper.

A window in the cottage opened, revealing the gnarled face of an old man.

"Come in at once!" he called out. "Shut the door behind you, and mind you don't be lettin' in any of those confounded beasts either." He banged the window shut again.

Meryl turned to Halstatt, who still had his hands over his ears. "Shall we?" she asked.

"Eh?" he replied.

She snorted and said, "Come on, we're going in."

It was more difficult than may be supposed to get in without admitting any cats. They swarmed the door, yowling and clawing at the door frame and the travellers' legs. Halstatt resorted to kicking at them, which made Meryl furious; she had always been rather fond of cats.

When they finally managed to squeeze through, they found themselves in a surprisingly bright common room, more like a workshop than a dwelling. It was full of sawdust. A thick golden powder lay on every surface: the large wooden table in the centre of the room strewn with various tools, the low stools by the hearthfire and the six chairs that were stacked in pairs by the wall. Motes danced in the sunbeams that streamed in through the side windows, which were tall rectangles of thick glass set in heavy wooden frames, hinged to open outward, like small doors.

The old man stood bent over a lathe, which was powered by a foot pump. He was humming tunelessly to the rhythm of the pumping as he artfully chiselled off a curled wood shaving. Meryl thought he looked like a gnome, or an ancient elf. She watched in fascination as a rectangular block on the lathe was magically transformed into a delicate pillar. The gnome added some finishing touches and then stepped off the foot pump. When the lathe had slowly spun to a stop he turned and scrutinized his company.

His eyes were dark brown and squirrel-bright, his expression solemn and difficult to read. He looked at them steadily before saying, "I'll be guessin' that you've not come for the chairs, then."

"No," replied Meryl, "we're travellers on our way west."

"Ah," said the little man. Then he turned his gaze upon the draoi, where it rested for several moments.

"This is Halstatt. He's a draoi. I'm Meryl, a mabinog. We're going to find Avalon." She bit her lip, realizing how strange she sounded.

"Ah," said the man again. Then he bowed to them both. "I'm honoured to make your acquaintance. I am Pedr O'Brien, master carpenter. And I think that it might be well to have a seat by the hearth while I bake us a bannock." He pointed the way.

The small stools they sat upon were exquisite, though simple in design. Meryl thought that they were the first real stools that she had seen in her life; everything else was just a shabby imitation. Pedr mixed up the bannock quickly and put it on the fire to bake, then joined them on a third stool. He was obviously a man who thought before he spoke, because he gazed at them again in silence until Meryl began to fidget.

"A draoi," he said abruptly. Then he was silent once more.

"Indeed, indeed," replied Halstatt.

For the first time Meryl noticed how uncomfortable her companion looked. She wondered whether carpenters made him nervous; he did look very much like a tree, after all. Then she noticed the suspicious manner in which he was eyeing the fire, drawing his twiggy elbows and root-like toes in close to his body. The realization that he was afraid of the flames cheered her up; for once Halstatt was too preoccupied to monopolize the conversation.

"My father told me he met one of your kind, back home in Eire. He was a lad, then," volunteered Pedr. Halstatt nodded, but didn't reply.

"There is a draoi there, Halstatt told me," Meryl responded. Silence descended again. "He talks to numskulls," she added desperately.

That drew both pairs of eyes to her. Halstatt's were horrified. "I said no such thing, *hruumph-nha*, indeed I did not!" he declared hotly.

"Yes, you did," Meryl retorted. "When we first met, you told me to go talk to the draoi in Eire who was used to talking to numskulls. Don't tell me you've forgotten?" she said, with wide-eyed innocence.

"Of course I haven't forgotten," Halstatt snapped. "I'm only sorry now that you didn't take my advice and leave at once, *hruumph-nha*." He turned to Pedr and began to apologize profusely. "You must excuse her, indeed, indeed. She's just left the Hall and she's only been in my company for a few days now. I haven't had time to correct her manners. I'm sure that your father was anything but a numskull, indeed, indeed, and must have been a very wise fellow to seek out a draoi." He turned back to Meryl and glared at her. She only grinned in response.

Pedr watched the exchange with interest. "You're a mabinog," he said to Meryl then.

Halstatt snorted but didn't speak.

"Yes, I am." She threw Halstatt an angry look.

"Then I'm supposin' you've paid your respects to Aiobhell at my door."

Meryl stared at him blankly. Ayvell, it sounded like. Did he mean one of the cats? What did they have to do with being a mabinog?

"Not properly," sniffed Halstatt. "That would be a fault of her manners again, *hruumph-nha*."

"You know this ... Ayvell?" Meryl asked, puzzled. "I didn't see anyone at the door."

Halstatt turned to Pedr and said, "You see why she was forced to leave the Hall. Her education there was sorely lacking, I'm afraid." He turned back to Meryl and said, in his most pompous draoi voice, "The statue of the harpist is Aiobhell. She was a renowned ruler in Eire, the guardian of the O'Brien clan, and a famed musician. Really, it's astonishing that the Hall didn't tell you anything about her, *hruumph-nha*."

"A famed harpist and ruler? Then why haven't I learned of her?" Meryl asked incredulously. It seemed unlikely that the Hall would neglect such an honourable figure.

"Well, I suppose they think that she gives them a bad name. Ridiculous human nonsense, of course." The draoi looked down his nose at Meryl and then began to pick fastidiously at the warm, flat bannock that Pedr had set before them.

"Why?"

Pedr gave a low laugh, like an old owl chuckling in the night. "Scared of her, no doubt. And well they should be — she's a fierce guardian."

"In what way?"

Halstatt brushed the crumbs delicately from his lips and answered her. "There is a legend," he began sternly, "that says when you heard Aiobhell playing upon her harp you didn't live to tell about it."

Meryl's jaw dropped. "You mean she killed you?"

"In a manner of speaking, *hruumph-nha*. As usual you've jumped to hasty human conclusions. She didn't come after her listeners with poison or her brother's axe, or anything so messy, indeed, indeed. It is said that her music was simply so beautiful that people died of joy when they heard it. Of course, that would be a comfortable way to die, if dying was your goal, but it's rather an unfortunate conclusion to a concert. You soon have no audience, if you see what I mean, *hruumph-hruumph-nha*."

Pedr laughed again, and leaned over to Meryl. "All Art be powerful, my dear, not just Aiobhell's. It claims you, and rules you. You become its servant, bound to do the bidding of your craft. Remember that, as you journey."

"That sounds like what Darren said," Meryl breathed.

"Truth be always the same," Pedr replied. He bit off some bannock and chewed pensively.

When they had finished eating, Pedr rose and opened the door. Cats of all descriptions swarmed into the room. From a small pantry at the rear of his cottage Pedr procured a large jug of milk, which he poured into a long, low trough against the far wall. When the cats had settled down to feed, Meryl counted thirty-one tails in total. The sight enchanted her so much that she pulled her harp from her sack and composed a song on the spot.

Puss set out into the gloaming,
Heart and mind intent on roaming,
His eyes shone grim within the dim,
While the wind commenced a'moaning.

The owls blinked bleary tawny eyes,
Bats pierced the gloom with shrilling cries,
Puss trod along and purred a song,
Though clouds tore ragged 'cross the skies.

The restless dead arose to walk,
The fearful folk their doors did lock,
Yet Puss went on, his courage strong,
For cowardice his soul did mock.

The wolves howled long into the chill,
And stoats slid silent to their kill,
Puss flexed his claws within his paws,
And stalked his phantom quarry still.

On through the shadows of the moon,
Sir Puss did prowl as though 'twere noon,
His bristled fur did onward spur,
His murky foes to flee and swoon.

Aurora woke and darkness fled,
The fox skulked homewards to his bed,
Puss home returned, no bridges burned,
And tamely let himself be fed.

She finished her song with a flourish. It didn't really suit either the mood or the style, but she couldn't help herself; she was quite pleased with her inspiration.

Halstatt merely *hruumph-nha*-ed into his chin, but Pedr clapped and smiled. The cats had finished their meal and began to move about the cottage. One enormous tabby leaped up onto Pedr's lap and added his purr to the quiet plucking of the harp strings. The music was interrupted when a calico queen jumped onto Meryl, but the mabinog didn't mind. She wanted to know more about their curious host.

"Avalon," said Pedr, as he gazed pensively into the fire. "Now that is a name I've not heard in many a long year."

"Do you know any stories about it? Where it may be located, even?" Meryl asked eagerly.

"Oh, I know snatches of plenty of tales. Some stories say it's the home of the old gods, some that it's the source of wisdom, others that it's the realm where poets truly belong. Most legends I've heard say that any person who travels there becomes more than mortal, as it is the land of the ever-living. As for where it's located, well, I can tell you this. There was a man lived in my village when I was a lad, and rumour said that he had been there, to the land of endless summer."

Meryl suppressed a cry of delight and leaned forward in her chair. "Where? Did he ever say where it was?"

Pedr stroked his chin and looked at the young girl thoughtfully. "Oh, he said plenty of it, he did, but most of it was beyond anyone's understanding."

"What do you mean?" asked Meryl.

"He was mad," Pedr replied bluntly.

"Mad!"

"He left the village as a young man, his heart full ready for adventures, folk said. He was gone for an age — so long that all believed him dead, and his own mother keened for him. But when I was no more than a babe he returned. It took a fair while before folk knew who he was, that changed was he. He was wild, and raved on about the mists that surround the Summer Land, how they burn with their chill."

"So he was never there after all," Meryl said, disappointed.

"Now why be you thinkin' that?"

"Well, he was a madman. You can't trust what he said."

Pedr stroked his chin again before responding. "It was his madness that made folk believe him in the end. And it was his madness that earned him our pity."

Meryl felt increasingly confused. "What do you mean?"

"There's a story says that if you drink from Ceridwen's cauldron you'll become a bard," Pedr began.

"I know that!" Meryl interrupted. "That's part of the reason why I want to find Avalon!"

"Truly," said Pedr. "Then you'd best hear the whole of it. For the legend goes on to say that anyone unworthy of the craft who drinks from the cauldron grows mad, and is doomed to rave for the rest of her days."

"Oh," said Meryl.

"Oh, indeed, indeed," added Halstatt. For the first time that evening he began to look truly cheerful.

"Aye," said Pedr, "so we pitied him, for it was a sorrow to see one who hoped for so much and achieved so little."

Meryl shivered, in spite of the heat from the fire. Insanity! What a horrible fate. If they ever did reach Avalon she wondered if she'd be willing to take such a risk.

Pedr smiled at her. "Take heart, lass. In all his ravings the poor man spoke one thing clearer than the rest. Avalon can be found only by those the guardians grant permission to. For all others, the island is invisible and the surrounding land barren."

"How will that help us find it?" Meryl complained.

"If they wish you to, you will, lass, never fear for that. A quest such as yours rarely goes unanswered."

They talked on into the night: about Halstatt's magical rose, about the Hall and about the journey. Meryl told the story of Darren and showed Pedr her rose clasp; he was impressed by the work.

"A Master made this," he said, holding it respectfully.

Meryl threw a triumphant look at Halstatt, who merely yawned in return. Pedr took this as a cue. He got up and turned all the cats outside, then banked the fire for the night and vanished into his small room at the back.

The travellers made their beds with the soft woollen blankets Pedr provided. Meryl laid hers on the hearth, snuggling in the warmth thrown off by the coals, while Halstatt placed his on the other side of the room. He claimed it was too hot next to the fire, but Meryl suspected he was afraid of sparks igniting him while he slept. He fell asleep quickly, pulling his roots up to his chin and wrapping his branchy arms around them. The room was soon filled with his chirping snores, but Meryl lay awake, staring at the red coals. The story of the madman had upset her. Avalon had seemed like such a wonderful place, like a promised land. Now it was tainted with danger. She shivered, remembering the "burning mists," and fell into a fitful sleep.

CHAPTER SEVEN

S UNSHINE AND THE MEWLING of thirty-one hungry cats woke Meryl. Pedr greeted her cheerfully.

"It's well you're awake, then. The folk have been and gone for their chairs, and left some good fresh bread for our breakfast. I'll fetch some cheese from the back as well, but you'll have to mind it until I've fed the cats."

Mind it she did, fighting off the hungry beasts until Pedr appeared again with the large jug of milk. When the cats had settled, they sat down to their own meal, Meryl first having to go fetch Halstatt from the woods. He had fled there to avoid being seen by the strangers.

"Too many humans at once gives me chilblains, *hruumph-nha*," he said, as he took his seat as close as he dared to the hearth. Meryl pointed out that he was happy enough for the food they'd left behind. Halstatt simply grunted and continued eating.

Meryl didn't want to leave, but they hadn't much choice. It was fine to presume on hospitality for one night as travellers, but they could hardly expect more. Pedr would want to get back to his work and not have to worry about entertaining anyone. All the same, she didn't want to go without learning something of his craft from him first. "Halstatt said I needed to find Masters," she thought to herself. "I'll have to try."

"Pedr," she said tentatively, "may I stay and watch you work for a while? Or even help you in some way, to pay you for your kindness? It would mean a great deal to me." She looked at him hopefully.

Pedr gazed back at her, rubbing his chin thoughtfully with

his strong, coarse hand. "I could use some help with the wood," he said.

Meryl grinned delightedly.

They went out to a shed behind the house. It had no windows, so they had to bring a lantern and leave the door open. It was warm and dark, the dry air pungent with the rich smell of lumber. Boards were stacked in rows, according to their different lengths and thicknesses. The thicker blocks were individually wrapped in sacking and piled together according to type. There was cedar in the near right corner; Meryl could smell it the moment she stepped into the shed. The sweet, rich scent brought back a flood of memories of the Hall and her mother. The sudden force of her emotions made her gasp.

"Powerful, isn't it?" Pedr said proudly.

"Very," said Meryl. She tried to keep the tears from affecting her voice, but failed.

"What be the matter then, lass?" Pedr asked gently.

Meryl ducked her head, took a deep breath, then looked up. "It's silly, I guess. The smell of cedar — my mother had a cedar trunk she kept her clothes in, made from a tree that was struck down in a storm. I remember her having to tell me that it wasn't wrong to have the trunk, because it scared me. I'd always been told that bards never destroyed a sacred tree, and I thought she had killed the cedar. Her clothes always smelled like it, afterwards. Oh, well ..." she finished lamely.

"She be gone then, your mother?"

Meryl nodded. "She died of a summer fever, a year ago. I haven't cried about it for a long time."

"It's right to cry for those you miss, lass. I still weep for my Da, every now and then, when I be in the forest on a warm summer morning. I can see him touching the trees, bidding them good morrow, and asking their permission to take one of their number. Very fond of the trees was my Da." He smiled at her gently.

His story made her curious, and she forgot her grief. "Your father talked to the trees? I thought I was the only person who did that." She'd never told anyone that she talked to trees before, but if Pedr had seen his father do it he might not think she was crazy.

"Oh aye, my Da talked to them regular, as do I. Trees be the wisest creatures on the earth." He began to sort through a pile of oak, looking each piece over carefully and rewrapping it gently before going on to the next. Finally, in the back of the shed, he found what he wanted. It looked like a branch, or the main limb of a large shrub. Meryl couldn't imagine why he'd choose it over all the wonderful boards he'd examined, but she supposed he knew what he was doing. They went out into the sunshine and closed the door behind them.

"Was your father a carpenter like you?" Meryl asked, once they were back in the cottage. She spoke quietly so as not to waken Halstatt, who was napping by the hearth. Normally she might have taken delight in poking him awake, but now she was grateful for the chance to talk to Pedr alone.

"Nay, he was a woodcutter was my Da. He used to take me into the forest and show me the trees growing there, in all their strength. He taught me how to choose the trees for cutting, taking only the ones whose passing would be a help to the others, giving them more air to breathe and room to grow, you see. We'd never be cutting in the same place too often, either. He'd rage when he'd see areas cleared of trees by cutters with no respect for the forest. We'd always plant new trees in those spots, and he'd guard them carefully to make sure that they got a good start on life."

As he talked he shaved the bark and rough spots off the wooden pole, working quickly, his hands almost caressing the wood as they sought out the places that needed smoothing. The gentle *shnick, shnick* of the blade on the wood was so soothing that Meryl might have fallen asleep too if it hadn't been for the story.

"So you worked as a woodcutter like him?"

"Aye, for many years. I felt as though I were a tree myself, I came that close to them. And then it seemed that when I touched the wood I could feel the thing inside, be it a chair, or a spinning wheel, or a statue like Aiobhell out there. I took to carving in the evenings, and soon I was good enough that the local carpenter said he'd take me on as an apprentice. I was happy to go, though I sorely missed being with my Da in the woods." He felt along the wood, seemed satisfied, then chose a new blade to work with. He began to carve the pole, beginning from the bottom.

"How did you come to be here?" Meryl asked.

Pedr grunted. "There's a tale, though not entirely a happy one. Eire fell on troubled times, some decades ago. Da died, and life seemed sour in my village. I wanted to go far away, put my troubles behind me." He paused and looked up at her knowingly. "Troubles follow, though. You'll be finding that yourself, if you've any." He went back to his carving. "I found my way here, and was welcomed. Aiobhell came from a nearby tree to guard me — storm-struck, like your mother's. This has been my home for many a year now. Folks know me, and keep me busy."

"And the cats?" Meryl asked, smiling.

"Ah, the cats," he chuckled. "The cats know me, too, and tell any wandering strays, I'll warrant. It be home for them, as well."

Meryl looked over at Halstatt, sleeping peacefully by the hearth. "I think I'll go into the forest and practise," she said. "He's grumpy if I wake him, and makes rude comments about my playing."

Pedr smiled at her. "Don't be minding his comments, lass. I think he likes your playing well enough. I know I found it a fair treat, and sure I am that I heard the pussycats caterwauling that song of yours to the moon, last night. You just keep practising, lass."

Meryl thanked him, grabbed her harp and left the cottage.

The forest was so quiet, and her mind so full of the story of Pedr's father, that she wandered about for a while just making friends with the trees. She practised, and then started working on a "tree song," but her muse was far away. She ambled back to the cottage several hours later, still puzzling over the tune.

In the cottage she found Halstatt perched on a stool, watching Pedr work with the same fascination she had felt earlier. She came nearer to see what he'd done with the pole.

"Just in time," Pedr said with a smile, and he held it out for her inspection. It was exquisite. A winding vine had been carved up the length of the pole, reaching to an open rose bloom at the head.

"It's yours," Pedr said, "inspired by your quest. I wanted to add my own good luck to your friend's. I heard a tale once of a traveller who walked great distances with such a staff, and it brought him safely to rest."

"It's a walking stick," Halstatt said solemnly.

Meryl took the staff and ran her fingers over it. There were intricate leaves, buds and thorns carved in relief along the vine. What amazed her was that it was so smooth to the touch, despite all the work. She held it upright, jabbing the bottom lightly into the floor. It was sturdy, and exactly the right height. Looking at Pedr she said, "It's so beautiful. What kind of wood is it?"

"Hawthorn," the carpenter replied. "Some folks say it's a sacred tree, and other folks call it unlucky, though to my mind they're just uncomfortable 'round about holy things. In any case, it's a relative of the rose, and I'm hoping it will keep your step sure."

"I can't believe you made it in so little time," she marvelled. She thought about her unfinished song.

"Time is what it is," Pedr said cryptically. Seeing her puzzlement he explained. "I've been carving since I was a lad, for nigh on six decades now. The time it took for me to learn that work was a lifetime, lass. Remember that, when you find your Summer Land, and Ceridwen's cauldron sits before you. It be a powerful drink that gives a lifetime in a moment."

Meryl didn't know what to say to that; it sounded uncomfortably like what Halstatt had told her. "Thank you, for all your kindness," she mumbled.

She collected her things and the pair made their farewells. Meryl remembered to pay her respects to Aiobhell this time.

"Well, that was certainly a pleasant human being, indeed, indeed," said Halstatt sociably as they walked west along the forest path. "Though certainly he could have done with fewer cats."

CHAPTER EIGHT

THE RAIN PELTED DOWN, running in little rivulets beneath the collar of Meryl's cloak. She tried to make the best of the situation and not complain, but by noon she was completely drenched. Finally she called a halt, found shelter beneath the trees and built a fire. Halstatt muttered, "It's about time, indeed, indeed," but Meryl was too busy trying to get warm to snap back at him.

They were a gloomy pair. Meryl wished herself back at the Hall; even scripting would be preferable to shivering in the rain. Halstatt spluttered and hissed, moaning about his deserted moss patch. It was hard to tell what made him more uncomfortable, his dampened state or his closeness to an open fire. To both of them, Avalon had come to seem like a distant dream, or a child's tale. Instead of letting up, the rain began to pour in earnest, and they stirred themselves to build a makeshift shelter. It wasn't much drier, but it protected the fire enough to get a cheery blaze going. Meryl felt her spirits lift.

"When do you think we'll come to the next village?" she asked the draoi sociably.

Halstatt shuffled closer to the fire and then jumped back as a spark landed and sizzled on his knee. "I don't know," he snapped. "All I want to do is find Avalon, fetch my rose and be back at my moss patch before the first frost. Then you can stumble about all of Albaine, and Eire too, indeed, indeed, and explore to your heart's content, *hruumph-hruumph-nha.*" He sneezed and sidled up to the fire once again.

"Fair enough," Meryl replied calmly. "Though finding Avalon will be no easy task. We can't simply wander about the west country until we run into some magical mists. There must be a direct way there — we just need to find it."

"Well, of course there's a Way there, there's a Way to all the magical places of Albaine, *hruumph-nha*. It's finding the Way that's the trouble, indeed, indeed. Didn't they teach you anything useful at the Hall?"

Meryl bit her tongue to keep from snapping back, but failed. "Fine then," she answered, "as soon as the rain lets up we'll search for a village and ask the first person we meet for directions to the nearest magical road. Hopefully we'll reach Avalon in time for supper tomorrow." With that she rolled herself up in her cloak and turned her back on the draoi.

There was a weighty silence between them for several minutes, until Halstatt broke it with an apologetic snort. "There's a Way not far from here if I'm not mistaken, and I'm usually not when it comes to magical things, indeed, indeed."

Meryl spun around to face him. "You mean that there really are special paths to magical places, that there is even one nearby, and you waited until now to tell me? Do you prefer tromping blindly about the forest?" She glared furiously at the draoi.

"As a matter of fact, I do, indeed, indeed. As would you if you knew anything about the Ways, *hruumph-nha*, so don't vent your spleen on me, if you please." He glared back at Meryl.

She tried to speak calmly. "Fine, then. Tell me about these magical Ways."

Halstatt assumed as much of his pompous teaching expression as he could in spite of his numerous sneezes. "The Ways are the fairy roads that connect all their dwellings and dancing greens. Very sensibly, they prefer them to those horrid, dusty versions made by you humans, *hruumph-nha*."

"But why didn't you say this earlier, Halstatt? We could have been in Avalon by now," Meryl interrupted.

"Eggs and evergreens, weren't you listening? They're the roads of the Twlwyth Teg, and they don't take kindly to having strangers, especially human strangers, stomp all over them. They're apt to get very churlish, indeed, indeed."

"The roads are?" Meryl asked, puzzled.

"Not the roads, the Twlwyth Teg! Goodness, you're thick at times."

Meryl pointedly ignored this last comment. "But the Twlwyth Teg are supposed to be kind to people, aren't they? The Hall's cook used to leave milk for them every night, and she always got a present in return. She called them the 'good people' and always spoke of them as her friends."

"Oh, indeed, indeed, the common jabberings of the human being are as exact about fairies as they are about draoi, no doubt, no doubt indeed." Halstatt sniffed. "The Twlwyth Teg have no cares. They don't care if you live, and they don't care if you die. Of course they'll pay you for some milk, but they're just as likely to lure you into a bog if they think it's worth a laugh, *hruumph-nha*. They endure humans while they find them useful, but they react quickly to being annoyed, and finding a human on one of their Ways is very annoying to them, indeed, indeed."

"You mean they'd hurt me?" Meryl asked.

"They'd likely curse you," Halstatt replied easily. "But as you're a would-be bard they might just drag you along to a fairy ring and dance with you for fifty years or so. It's rather nice for humans, though far too hectic for a draoi, if you see what I mean."

"Dancing for fifty years doesn't sound overly nice to me, either. I should think a person would drop dead from exhaustion."

"Oh no, not until afterwards. It all goes by in an instant for the dancer, indeed, indeed it does. Only when you stop and take a bite to eat, you crumple into black dust. That's the trouble of it all — it's not what you'd call a fulfilling life, even by human standards, *hruumph-nha*."

"Oh dear," responded Meryl.

"Yes, that's rather what I thought you'd think," Halstatt replied cheerfully.

Meryl chewed on her fingernails while she considered the danger. "Are there always fairies on the Ways?" she finally asked.

Halstatt *hruumph-nha*-ed and looked worried. "That's what you can't be sure of," he said. "They travel in groups, visiting each of their magic places during the summer. If they're dancing on a green you can be fairly safe on the Ways, indeed, indeed, but if they're moving around ..."

"Ah," said Meryl. "I don't suppose you can tell when they're on the Way, can you?"

"Not before I'm on it I can't, and then it's rather too late, if you see what I mean."

"I do." Meryl sighed hopelessly. Then she perked up again. "Halstatt, would they hurt you? You're a draoi, after all. Don't they respect you?"

Halstatt appeared to grow quite uncomfortable. "Yes, well, you'd think that would be the case, wouldn't you?" He tried to busy himself with brushing ashes off his arms.

"Halstatt?"

"Hmmm?"

Meryl stared him down. "Halstatt, there's something you're not telling me, isn't there?"

Halstatt mumbled and then threw up his arms. "Draoi don't like the Twlwyth Teg," he said fiercely.

"Why?"

Halstatt chewed his lower lip. "They mock us," he answered dismally.

"Mock you?"

"They pull out our leaves, and snap off our fingers and toes, and they call us horrible names."

"Names?" said Meryl. She was finding it hard not to smile.

"Names — like 'moss-mind' and 'bark-brain.' It's really most insulting, indeed, indeed. I'd rather we didn't discuss it any longer if you please." He looked so doleful that Meryl choked back her laughter.

They sat in silence for a while, until Meryl felt the draoi had recovered his sense of dignity.

"So there's a Way close by. Will it take us to Avalon?" she inquired.

"Eventually, indeed, indeed it will. Of course it might lead us on a trek all over the magical places of fairyland, and we're sure to run into some of the Twlwyth Teg if that happens, *hruumph-hruumph-nha*."

"Can't we just walk beside the Way?"

He turned and stared at her. "My figs and fingers, you really do know shockingly little," he said. Meryl clenched her fists and suppressed a growl. "The Ways are found on common soil but they don't follow it. They're in fairyland." With this he waved his hand vaguely about him, as though trying to swat a fly.

"I don't understand."

"Ah, well, there it is. There's your Hall education for you. No wonder you came to me, no wonder, indeed, indeed. It's very straightforward. You can only follow a Way when you're on it. If you're not on it, it takes its own path and you take yours. It's a puzzle, I'll grant you, but then most magical things are to you humans." He looked on her pityingly.

Meryl had to agree with him; the mystery of the Ways was beyond her understanding. She decided not to worry about it.

"Halstatt, is there any chance that you can jump on a Way and see where it goes, and then jump back off it before any fairies catch you?"

He didn't look thrilled at the suggestion, but he considered it anyway. "I could try, you know," he replied. "I'm not promising anything, indeed, indeed I'm not, but I could try."

"Good!" Meryl exclaimed. "We'll try in the morning. We'll be true Wayfarers then!" she joked cheerfully.

Halstatt simply grunted in reply and rubbed his twiggy fingers protectively.

CHAPTER NINE

IT POURED RAIN ALL NIGHT and into the next morning. The fire had died out in the night and they were unable to get it started again, so breakfast was a silent and disgruntled affair. Cold and miserable, they were soon tromping woefully through the wet forest. Halstatt would have to stop every so often to get a fresh sense of the location of the Way. He had caught a dreadful cold, and it seemed to affect his ability to sniff out the magic. Between his cold, the rain, and his dread of the fairies he was a surly companion. Meryl found herself biting her tongue so often she was amazed it had not dropped off.

Finally he halted abruptly. "It's here," he said.

"Are you on it now?" Meryl asked anxiously. She looked around for fairies.

"Of course not. You can still see me, can't you? Ferns and fiddleheads, I believe I shall lodge a complaint with the Hall concerning the quality of its education when this is all over, indeed, indeed." He sneezed violently.

"Don't get started about that," Meryl snapped. "Just jump on the Way and see if it goes to Avalon."

"And get my fingers torn off, no doubt, no doubt indeed," he snapped back. And the next moment he vanished. It was immediate; suddenly he was no longer there.

"Halstatt?" called Meryl, anxiously. "Halstatt, can you hear me?"

The only response was the dull thud of rain on the leaves overhead.

Meryl waited. Minutes crept by. Eventually she sat down on a log. It was old and rotting and not very pleasant to sit upon.

She pulled her cloak close about her body. "I hope I don't have to wait fifty years," she mumbled to a nearby oak. "I certainly hope Halstatt hasn't lost all his fingers," she added.

An hour passed, and Meryl began to doze, despite the strain of waiting. Finally she could stand it no longer. She walked to the spot where Halstatt had last stood and looked around. All she could see was the forest. She sniffed, checking whether or not she could smell the magic, but her nose had become as stuffed up as the draoi's. She thumped her walking stick on the ground and bellowed "Open up!" A crow squawked indignantly and flapped away. She searched her memory for fairy spells, all to no avail. Finally she spun around three times and thumped the ground again —

— And found herself on a brilliant sunny road of well-packed dirt, bordered on either side with green pastures. She was so startled that it was a moment before she saw the laughing band of tiny people. The tallest of them was no more than three feet in height, the smallest of them a good foot shorter than that. They were human-like in shape, all of them slender, long-limbed and finely featured. Their movements were so quick and delicate that they made Meryl think of butterflies, though they were far more fluid and graceful than any insect; every gesture they made seemed to be part of an intricate dance. Their laughter was like harp music and birdsong perfectly blended. She immediately understood how people in stories became entranced by their voices.

The most significant element of their appearance, however, was their colour. They were blue. Their long, thick hair was a deep blue-black, gleaming like a raven's wing in the sunshine. Their skin was blue, a pale-sky tint that flushed a darker shade in their lips and cheeks. Even their clothes were a brilliant cobalt colour, made of some diaphanous fabric that floated and shimmered, like their hair. The females wore long flowing gowns that did nothing to hamper their movements but which swirled around them with the lightness of swan's down. The males wore breeches and tunics and soft navy-blue leather boots that came up to their knees and were pointed at the toes.

The group swarmed about a bush in the centre of the road. A second look revealed the bush to be Halstatt, squatting with his hands over his head and moaning piteously.

"Come, honest fern friend, tell us a riddle," a fairy cried, giving one of Halstatt's hands a tug. One of his fingers snapped off and the draoi howled.

Meryl leapt towards the group, her staff held before her. "Leave him alone!" she bellowed.

All the fairies spun to look at her, their smiles broadening wickedly at the prospect of fresh fun. "A mortal!" several cried. "A mortal on the Way! Here's a game, indeed."

They began to advance towards her. A quick count revealed twelve in their number. Meryl gulped and brandished her staff once more. "Get back," she said, in as threatening a voice as she could muster. But the group merely laughed and continued to advance.

"Halstatt!" Meryl shrieked. "Halstatt, get us out of here!"

The laughter of the fairies grew louder. They drew about her in a ring, obscuring her vision of the draoi. "Shall we dance?" a male fairy asked mockingly.

"I'd rather not," Meryl replied, to much laughter.

Suddenly one of the fairies, a female, shrieked and pointed towards Meryl's neck. The others looked and began shrieking as well, running about and into one another in confusion. "Iron! Iron! Iron on the Way!" they bellowed. Meryl reached up and touched her rose clasp in wonder. Halstatt appeared at her side, looking strangely bald. "I'd forgotten that," he said. "I've never forgotten anything before. It must come from associating with

humans, *hruumph-nha*. The Twlwyth Teg hate iron." He sniffled, looked at his broken fingers and moaned.

Meanwhile, the fairies had withdrawn into a whispering group, all of them glancing over at Meryl with wide, angry eyes.

"Halstatt, what does that mean?" Meryl whispered fiercely. "Are they going to curse us?" The thought gave her the shivers. Fairy curses could last nine generations; that much she had learned at the Hall.

He managed to draw his thoughts away from his missing fingers and considered the situation. "I don't know," he said slowly.

"What do you mean you don't know? You're a draoi, you're supposed to know these things."

"As I've said before," Halstatt replied icily, "draoi don't like fairies. We try not to think about them. We simply wish them to leave us alone, indeed, indeed. However, I believe that iron stops their spells. That's why they dislike it, if you see what I mean, *hruumph-nha*. It puts them in a very bad temper, if you'll pardon the pun."

Meryl looked at him blankly. He sighed and went on. "They don't want mortals on their Ways at the best of times, and a mortal with iron is a dreadful thing, indeed, indeed. Really, it's surprising you were able to get on the Way at all, wearing that rose. They're probably deciding what to do with you."

Meryl shivered again. "Halstatt, if my rose keeps their magic from working why don't we just leave now, before they do anything?"

Halstatt snorted. "Leave! Larks and lilypads, we can't leave now. We're stuck on this Way until they let us go."

"But if their magic won't work —"

"It's not them that's stopping us. It's the Way itself. The Ways do what the fairies ask them. And the Ways have no fear of iron, indeed, indeed they do not."

Morosely Halstatt began to rub his leafless head. Meryl was glad to see that he still had a few fingers left. She wondered how long it would take the others to grow back, but she knew that now wasn't the time to ask.

The fairies had apparently come to a decision. They approached the pair sombrely, with one of the taller males in front as a spokesman. He looked very stern indeed as he addressed them.

"You have committed a serious crime. Iron is not permitted on the Ways. It has never been done before. We have decided to take you to the fairy court and have you tried by our King."

Halstatt gave a small yelp. One of the female fairies came forward and solemnly tied their wrists together, though first she allowed Meryl to jury-rig a harness for her walking stick so that she could carry it across her back. Meryl thought that the rope the fairies used to bind them was ridiculously fine — more like a spider's web than anything else — but as she tried to pull her hands apart she discovered how terribly strong it was.

Once their prisoners were bound, the fairies began to process soberly down the road, pulling Halstatt and Meryl along behind them. The draoi looked more miserable than Meryl had seen him yet.

"Is it so very bad?" she whispered to Halstatt.

"It's worse than bad," he mumbled back.

"Oh dear, it seems I have a talent for committing heinous crimes and getting caught at them. Can it really be worse than the Council of Bards?" she asked hopefully.

He stared at her. "Snakes and snowflakes, Gwyn ap Nudd will make your Council look like a Beltaine picnic, indeed, indeed he will."

Gwyn ap Nudd. Meryl's heart stopped beating. "He's the King of the fairies?" She recognized the look on Halstatt's face.

"Now, don't start about the Hall again. Remember, I was behind a year's lessons when you met me."

"*Hruumph-hruumph-nha*, that's a poor excuse."

"I was told that Gwyn ap Nudd was a monstrous hunter who chased people into the land of Death with his pack of red-eared, red-eyed hounds."

Halstatt sniffed, then sneezed, then sniffed again. "Well, he is a hunter; he is King of the Otherworld; and he is King of the fairies. But if you're even one-eighth as wise as a newborn draoi you won't use the word 'monstrous' to describe him in the present company, indeed, indeed you won't. The water we're sitting in is hot enough already without you bringing it to a boil, if you see what I mean, *hruumph-nha*."

It seemed they walked a very long distance, always with the unvarying green fields on either side of the road. Initially, Meryl found nothing unusual about the Way. Then she noticed that the light never changed. At first she thought it was because there was never a cloud in the sky, which struck her as odd but not entirely unlikely; such days did occur in Albaine. So it came as a tremendous shock when she realized that the sun didn't move in the sky. Her shadow stayed the same length as it would normally be at high noon. Then the silence began to unnerve her. There were no birds. There was not even the sound of wind disturbing the grass in the fields. The air of the Ways was perfectly still, the light perfectly clear. It gave Meryl the impression that she was walking through the sky itself. She felt heavy, foreign. The strangeness frightened her, and she began to long for the journey to be over.

"What do I say to the King?" she whispered desperately to the draoi.

"As little as possible, and only the truth," he hissed back.

"This is hardly the time to start speaking in riddles," she grumbled. One of the fairies turned and barked at them to be silent before Halstatt had a chance to reply.

The troop stepped off the Way, drawing the prisoners with them. Meryl felt her feet leave the road. One of the fairies was steering her by the elbow but she didn't know how she was moving. She felt dizzy, as though she were tumbling, and she didn't feel right again until her feet touched firm ground in the middle of a broad, grassy circle, located in an oak grove. There were red fairies to her right, green fairies to her left, silvery-white fairies to the rear and the familiar blue fairies to the fore. When their own troop of captors bowed and stepped aside, Meryl was given a clear view of a large stone throne. The sight nearly made her faint, and all at once she wished the journey had been six times as long.

On the throne was a tall man — immense by fairy standards — wearing a long cloak of the same light, shimmering fabric patterned in diamonds of red, white, blue and green. He wore a golden crown upon his head, from which protruded a pair of antlers. He was dark, handsome, and very severe. Meryl was sure that the word "majestic" had been invented to describe him.

He spoke, and his voice was as deep and threatening as thunder. "Raindancer, why have you brought this mortal and this ..." he slowly looked over the draoi, "this tree-twin into our midst?"

The tall male fairy stepped forward. "We found them on the Way, your majesty." Gwyn ap Nudd made no response. "They were on the Way, my lord, and the mortal was discovered to be wearing this." He pointed to her clasp.

The fairy throng peered at Meryl's rose and then gasped. The King's face grew graver still, something Meryl hardly believed was possible. She was terrified. Halstatt moaned beside her, shaking so badly that his twigs rattled.

The King raised his hand and the tumult quieted. "Iron on the Way. Such a thing has never been heard of." His eyes bore into Meryl's. She wondered if he was expecting her to speak, and knew that she couldn't. "Why would you even attempt such a crime?" he demanded.

There was no doubt he expected an answer now. Meryl found the ghost of her voice hiding somewhere deep within her.

"If you please, my lord, I had no idea it was a crime," she squeaked.

"So, you plead ignorance?" His words rumbled across the grass towards her, nearly bowling her over. She didn't think that it was wise to answer either yes or no to the question. She bit her tongue and glanced desperately at the draoi.

He coughed and said, "Your majesty, the human is but a youngster, if you see what I mean, and has suffered greatly by a poor education, indeed, indeed she has."

"So then, your plea is that she's a fool?" the King interrupted.

Halstatt's eyes rolled in terror, and he merely spluttered in response.

Meryl felt a wave of anger sweep over her. "I'm neither a fool nor ignorant, if you please," she snapped. Halstatt tugged on her arm imploringly, but she brushed him aside. "I'm on a quest with my friend here, and we simply wanted to find the quickest route. I had no intention of spoiling your spells with my clasp. It's a gift from a friend and has nothing to do with fairies. Now, if you'll just untie us and point us towards Avalon we'll be on our way. Really, I think it's the least you can do after your people pulled out all my friend's leaves," she finished sternly.

A weighty silence followed her speech. Halstatt moaned quietly. Every face was still and flat; Gwyn ap Nudd's looked as though it were carved in stone.

"Avalon?" the King finally said. He sounded calm, at least.

"Yes, Avalon, if you please. My friend here had a rose that was stolen from him, and we think it might be there. At any rate, we think it came from there, so that might give us some clues." She wondered whether she should mention the cauldron of Ceridwen but decided that it was best to keep things simple.

"A rose?" queried the King. He looked distastefully at her clasp, but Meryl had the distinct feeling that his curiosity was piqued.

"A magical rose," Halstatt interrupted. Not even terror could keep him from bragging about his treasure. "It bloomed all year, indeed, indeed, and it was a gift of my mother's and so rather dear to me, if you see what I mean, *hruumph-nha*." He shut his mouth with a snap, suddenly afraid of saying too much.

"A magical rose," mused the King of the Twlwyth Teg. "That sounds a treasure indeed. But tell me," he said, turning suddenly back to Meryl, "have you decided to assist this bush-being on his quest out of the goodness of your heart, or the tediousness of your life, or do you have reasons of your own for travelling to the Summer Land?" His eyes pierced more sharply than any blade.

"Ah, well," stammered the mabinog, "you see, I've a quest of my own, and Halstatt is helping me. I mean, I am helping him as well, but, ah ..." Her voice trailed off.

"Well?" said the King. The coldness of his tone brought on another case of the shivers in Meryl, but she fought them off.

"You see, I'm on a quest to become a bard, and ..."

"Ah, yes," said the King, leaning back in his throne and studying her with amusement. It was rather like being a mouse observed at close quarters by a very large cat. "You wish to drink from Ceridwen's cauldron and instantly become a brilliant poet." The fairies laughed in malignant glee. Meryl felt her anger returning.

"I'm curious about the cauldron, yes. I want to see it, and maybe, maybe ..." here she glared at the draoi, who was too terrified to do anything but whimper in return, "as I said, maybe I'll drink from it. But I need to know about the rose as well. That's why I'm going to Avalon."

"And why do you need to know about the rose?" Gwyn ap Nudd's tone was still mocking.

"Because I do," she retorted. Halstatt stepped on her foot in horror, but the fury on the King's face was all she needed to mend her words. "Because I need to know if Taliesin stole it or not," she added weakly.

"You think it was Taliesin who stole this magical rose?" the King asked Halstatt.

"Yes, I do," the draoi replied firmly.

"And I'm convinced that if he did he had a good reason," Meryl added firmly.

"Taliesin," said the King. "We knew him well, as we know all who are born of the cauldron. He fled here as a child, trying to hide from Ceridwen herself. Of course it was pointless, but we found his antics highly diverting. He must have transformed himself into a dozen beasts before she finally caught him. After his bard-birth he became a frequent guest at our feasts. His stories about human follies were always amusing. Indeed, he was the only mortal who was granted freedom of travel on our Ways." He sat in silence and pondered. "I would hate to learn ill was thought of our friend, though what ill can be thought of playing a joke on a fern-fellow is a puzzle to us indeed."

Halstatt opened his mouth to protest, but Meryl spoke faster.

"The draoi are highly respected among my people," she said. "It would look very bad indeed if Taliesin were seen as a thief, much less a thief of an oracle he had befriended. But it also means a great deal to me," she added. "Taliesin is a hero of mine. If he didn't behave honourably, then, well ... I guess I don't know what I'll think of him then," she finished helplessly.

"Honour means much to us as well," said the King seriously. "The fact that you value it makes me think perhaps you did not mean to bring iron on our Way, for that is an act of great dishonour indeed."

Meryl asserted her innocence one more time. Gwyn ap Nudd seemed to listen with greater patience. And finally, after some silence, he spoke again.

"Leaflighter," he called to one of the red fairies, "how long has it been since one of our court has paid a visit to Avalon?"

"It's been four hundred years, my lord; not since you last courted the Queen," she replied. There was a general outbreak of laughter at this; even the King smiled.

"Ah, a long time indeed." He mused again in silence.

Meryl noticed that the entire court was leaning forward in anticipation. She felt her heart thump in her throat.

"Good," said Gwyn ap Nudd. "Leaflighter, you will accompany these two to Avalon. If the Queen accepts their questing, they may go. If she does not," he turned a granite smile on the pair, "then the draoi will be put to sea in a boat, and the girl ..." He paused in thought. Meryl saw his eyes note the shape of the harp in her sack. "Ah yes," he said coldly, "the girl will lose her voice. Thus we let the Queen of the Summer Land decide if the importance of their quest outweighs the measure of their offence."

Before either she or Halstatt could respond, Meryl felt herself struck with the same overwhelming confusion as before. When her head stopped spinning she found herself back on the Way, with the draoi and the red fairy.

"If you please," the fairy said politely, "I am Leaflighter, and Avalon is this way." She began walking down the fairy road.

Halstatt glared at Meryl, muttered, "Humans! Apples and anthills, preserve me from humans, *hruumph-hruumph-nha,*" and stomped off after the fairy.

Meryl wasn't sure whether she'd won a victory or sealed their doom.

CHAPTER TEN

L EAFLIGHTER PROVED to be a cheerful, chattery individual. She was one of the taller fairies, standing just over three feet in height. She had unusually pointed ears, even for a sprite, and large, slanted, amber eyes which, combined with her graceful walk, gave her the appearance of a cat. Her scarlet hair flew wildly about as she cavorted along the Way, until she finally braided it and stuck it up on her head, with the help of one of Halstatt's twiggy fingers. He yelped in angry protest when she nonchalantly pulled it off his hand, but she kept up such a steady stream of conversation that eventually he thawed towards her. Soon they were walking amiably together, while Meryl trailed woefully behind them.

It was hard to remain hopeless on the Way, however. Though the sun shone as brilliantly and steadily as before, there was a new freshness to the air, and sometimes one could hear snatches of distant, lovely music. Meryl even began to see flashes of vividly coloured flowers among the grass of the fields, which danced about in a gentle breeze. She began to wonder if the Ways reflected the mood of the fairies who walked on them. As they marched farther from the fairy court she felt her own spirits rising, despite the darkness of Gwyn ap Nudd's ruling. She raced to catch up to the others.

"Halstatt," she interrupted, "why did the King threaten to put you to sea in a boat?"

The draoi glared at her malevolently. "Ah, yes, I have yet to thank you for including me in your fairy punishment, *hruumph-nha*. That was very clever, indeed, indeed it was. Here was I, blithely thinking that I'd manage to escape with the loss of a few digits, and then you feel it necessary to open your mouth and flap your jaws to all the breezes of the earth."

"That's ridiculous. I found a way to escape punishment. All we have to do is get into Avalon and everything will be fine."

Leaflighter let loose a peal of merry laughter.

"Oh yes, you may laugh," Halstatt said sourly to the fairy. "It isn't you who faces exile and root rot, one can easily see that, they can indeed, *hruumph-nha*."

"Root rot?" asked Meryl.

"It's what happens to draoi when they can't feel the land beneath them. They lose their roots. It's a horrible thing. You can't imagine anything so bad."

"Not even a bard losing her voice?" Meryl replied heavily.

Halstatt opened his mouth to make a snide remark, caught Meryl's expression and thought better of it.

"Yes, well, that would be unfortunate," he muttered.

"But it isn't going to happen," Meryl insisted resolutely, once more eliciting the fairy's laughter. Both companions glared at her this time, but she remained unperturbed.

"Right," said Halstatt, "we're going to amble along the shore, looking for Avalon through the mist, and call out, 'If you please, we'd like to finish our quest, so would you be so kind as to send over a boat to fetch us? Then this good fairy, who's charged with seeing we arrive, can go off on her merry way.'" The draoi snorted and huffed at the idea.

"Why not?" Meryl said. "What else can we do?"

"Storks and starfish, not even a human could be so bold! We're talking of Avalon, not a village inn. The Queen has admitted only a handful of mortals, and only a few more draoi, since the beginning of time. It's her secret land, and she guards it jealously, if you see what I mean, *hruumph-nha*."

"No, I don't," snapped Meryl. "We've as much a right to quest there as anyone. Besides, if Pedr's mad village friend could go there, I don't see why we can't."

"You're very sure of yourself, mortal, aren't you?" Leaflighter commented. Her cat's eyes danced gleefully.

"You've no idea, indeed, indeed you don't," Halstatt groaned.

"The King enjoys a bit of boldness, else you would have been cursed unto the ninth generation long before now. Which would have been great fun," Leaflighter added cheerily. "I've always loved cursing humans. They howl so. But the Queen," the fairy tilted her head to one side in thought, "the Queen is as changing as the winds she controls. A bold step might gain you entrance, or it might shut her ears to your cries forever. There's no knowing the Queen's thoughts."

"But still, she's sure to find our quest interesting," Meryl argued. "And all the stories say that she's very kind to bards."

"True, but then you are no bard yet, mortal." Halstatt snickered at this, and Meryl thumped his shoulder. "And one should never presume to guess what might interest the Queen. The King has been trying since time began and has yet to solve the riddle."

"Well, we'll try," Meryl replied, as bravely as she could.

"Oh, we'll try," Halstatt agreed. "Though I can feel my toes shrinking from salt water already, indeed, indeed I can."

This ended all conversation for a time. They walked on for an hour or so, and then the fairy halted abruptly. An eager look crossed her face. "It's time to eat," she said suddenly, "and I think there's milk nearby."

She disappeared, leaving Meryl and the draoi gaping at the spot where she had just been standing.

"Well, if that isn't just lovely," he grumbled. "Now I suppose we simply have to hunker down here while she goes off chasing cows and pinching the noses of lazy milkmaids while they nap.

Hruumph-nha, if there's one race more thoughtless than humanity it must be the fairykind, indeed, indeed it must."

"Oh well, it gives us a break too. My legs are tired anyway." Meryl sat down on the Wayside.

The draoi joined her. "I don't suppose we have any of the honourable carpenter's food left?" he asked hopefully. The draoi had grown quite fond of human food. When he was rooted he didn't need to eat, and as he had been stationary for so long the novelty of food was still strong in him.

"No, we've nothing. Don't talk about it, you'll make me hungrier than I am already. Hopefully we'll get something when we arrive in Avalon."

"*Hruumph-nha.*" The draoi looked sceptical, but otherwise held his tongue.

"Halstatt, I'm sorry if I got you into trouble." It was her first admission of wrong-doing — a peace offering. The draoi looked very surprised. For a moment, a very brief moment, he was speechless.

"Ah, well, *hruumph-nha,* there you see, I don't really blame you. I said I'd jump on the Way, and so I did, knowing full well that fairies could be there. So the fault's my own, indeed, indeed."

"Yes, but I'm the one who jumped on it wearing iron. You'd never have been brought before the King if I hadn't meddled."

"Yes, well, there now, weren't you coming to my defence? And you saved most of my fingers and all of my toes, indeed, indeed you did, and grateful I am to you for that. Naturally if that ridiculous Hall of yours had given you any useful knowledge whatsoever you might have left the clasp behind, but then who's to say what would have happened then? A fifty-year dance, no doubt indeed, and only a pile of black dust to show for your efforts, if you see what I mean. No," he finished bravely, "I think that it's for the best, root rot and all."

"Thanks, Halstatt. You're a true friend." She threw her arms around the draoi, which made him splutter and cough and protest, but she thought he looked pleased nonetheless.

Leaflighter soon returned in high spirits; not that she could ever be accused of being unhappy at the worst of times. Halstatt was right about fairies not caring, Meryl thought to herself. "Have you pinched any noses?" she inquired politely.

"I have, indeed, indeed, as your illustrious pine-pal here would say," said Leaflighter, "and tipped over a few butter churns in the bargain."

Halstatt sniffed contemptuously. "Rootless, rootless," he muttered, much to Leaflighter's delight.

"Oh, the fun has only begun," Leaflighter said wickedly, and Meryl felt a strange sense of foreboding.

"You mean you're going back again? Shouldn't we be on our way to Avalon?"

"My, I've never met a mortal more eager to meet her doom," the fairy replied airily. "What's your hurry? There's some sport at hand to cheer us all. Avalon will wait."

"I'm hardly about to involve myself in some fairy high jinks, *hruumph-nha*," Halstatt replied stiffly.

"There's no sense arguing about it anyhow," Meryl cut in. "Until our fate's decided we can't get off the Ways."

"Oh no?" Leaflighter's expression grew sly.

The next moment the three were standing just inside the edge of the forest. Dusk had fallen, and the rain had finally stopped. Through the thinning trees Meryl could see the twinkle of lights.

"We're free!" she exclaimed, turning to Halstatt.

"Oh, hardly that," Leaflighter responded merrily. "The Way let you go because I told it to, but if you try to escape you'll find the fairy King's curse about your ears before you can sing a quarter note."

"What are you up to? We don't have time for this." Meryl felt herself growing hot with anger.

"Of course you do. What's an hour or two of fun? No journey is complete without it."

"I beg to differ, indeed, indeed I do," Halstatt said pompously. "Fairy fun is one thing we draoi have always been more than happy to do without. Fairy fun means the loss of one's fingers, toes, leaves and dignity. If you want fun, go find it. I'm staying here for a nice reasonable ponder, *hruumph-hruumph-nha*." With that the draoi sat down and stared stolidly at the tree across from him.

"Ah no, my leafy lad, that won't do at all," the fairy answered cheerfully. "We need you for the sport."

"We?" said Meryl. "I don't recall agreeing to be a part of your trick."

"Oh come now," Leaflighter said petulantly. "I've never met a more grumblesome pair in all my days. It's really very simple. There's a wedding dance in the village tonight and the mortals will be merrymaking. The drink's been flowing freely all evening. They'll believe anything they see tonight, however strange, however odd."

"Such as?" Meryl was curious in spite of herself.

"Such as the sudden appearance of three of their ancient gods — larger than life and a sight to behold!" Leaflighter shouted triumphantly.

The draoi and the human gaped at the fairy.

"Gods?" Meryl queried sceptically.

"Of course. You'll make a wonderful Danu, with the help of a little fairy magic, while I'll be Branwen — you can't have a wedding without the goddess of love, naturally. Our twiggy friend here will play Amaethon. He makes a very believable god of agriculture, don't you agree?" Leaflighter twinkled.

Halstatt began to splutter in horror and outrage. Meryl knew exactly how he felt.

"You want me to impersonate the mother goddess at a village wedding!?" she asked, hardly believing her ears. Leaflighter nodded happily. "Are you absolutely mad?"

The fairy shrugged. "If you prefer, I'll be Danu and you can be Branwen. I only suggested it the other way to be polite."

"Polite!" Meryl gasped. "How is it any better to be Branwen? Besides, no one believes in those old gods. They'll just think we're three lunatics from the forest."

"Oh, but that's where half the fun lies," Leaflighter crowed. "They'll suddenly be forced to believe all the old stories, and it will terrify them!"

"I don't see how that's any better," Meryl snapped. "They'll just be furious with us for making them look like fools once they learn the truth. We'll end up either on trial for blasphemy or finishing our days in a madhouse — or at least I will. You'll just vanish onto a Way and Halstatt will be sent back to the forest, happy as a fish in water. No thank you. If you want to play gods, you can play all by yourself."

"Now be reasonable," Leaflighter protested. "Whoever heard of a god wandering around on her own? They always travel in threes. Even mortals know that much."

"Even mortals know better than to run around pretending to be divinities," Halstatt said snidely. "It tends to make the existing divinities rather cross, if you see what I mean, *hruumph-nha.*"

"Nonsense!" Leaflighter giggled.

Before he could retort, the draoi found himself sprouting fresh foliage and growing in stature. Likewise, the fairy was transformed into a tall, flame-haired woman dressed in flowing red robes. Meryl alone remained the same. She gaped at her two companions; they certainly did appear to be godly.

Leaflighter looked at the mabinog in surprise. "Ah, the iron. I'd forgotten that. You'll have to take it off for me to change you."

"No, I certainly will not. I said that I'm not having any part of this joke and I meant it. Now change Halstatt back at once and take us to Avalon."

"No." Leaflighter pouted. "I'm not taking you anywhere if you're going to be so sour."

"You have to! Gwyn ap Nudd told you to take us to Avalon. You'll be in trouble if you don't do what he says."

"Ha! You know very little about fairies if that's what you think, mortal," Leaflighter said angrily. "If the King hears that you spoiled a joke he'll be angrier then ever with you; and I don't suppose you'll escape a curse the second time."

Halstatt pulled Meryl aside. "She means it," he hissed in her ear. He had to bend down from an astonishing height to do so. If Meryl hadn't known he was the draoi she would have found him terrifying. "Fairies are a temperamental lot, if you see what I mean."

"And gods aren't?"

"Well, they're wiser, and tend to be patient with fairies."

"We're not fairies."

"Thank heavens, no. But divine beings also tend to be lenient towards adventurers. We'd best just play the joke and be done with it."

"I don't see why. As long as I'm wearing iron she can't hurt me."

"Yes, well, there you see, I'm not wearing any iron, now, am I? *Hruumph-nha.*"

Meryl glared at Halstatt and the fairy in turn. "I think you're enjoying this," she said to the draoi, fiercely.

Halstatt spluttered but didn't deny the charge. In all honesty he liked the idea of playing Amaethon. Legends said that the god had a special soft spot for the draoi-folk. Some even said that it was Amaethon who created the twiggy-people in the first place.

"All right," Meryl snapped, unpinning the clasp. "I'll do it. But we'd better be done in half an hour and back on the Way to Avalon."

"But of course," Leaflighter replied sweetly, once again all smiles.

Meryl felt a sudden strangeness, and she imagined that she heard the same distant strains of music that were on the Way. When she looked down at herself she was astonished to see that she had grown at least a foot, had long, raven tresses falling over her shoulders and down to her waist, and was dressed in robes of a deep blue colour.

"There," the fairy said merrily, "that's far better. Though I think your staff would be better off with our Amaethon here. It's more of an agricultural symbol."

"Fine," replied Meryl, handing over the staff. She hated to admit it, but now she also felt excited. In a funny way, she was almost looking forward to the joke; it would make a great story to tell one day. "Do you suppose I can put my clasp back on?" she asked anxiously. "I can't lose it. It's my totem, you see."

"Try it," Leaflighter said. Meryl did so, and the spell held. "There now — we look a royal group indeed. Let's go."

"Wait, if you please," Halstatt said nervously. "Just exactly what are we going to do at this wedding?"

"Oh, the usual thing," Leaflighter said airily. "Make a grand entrance to the village hall and offer our blessings upon the couple — I'll do most of the speaking, naturally. Then, after they've all bowed down to us and fainted, we'll make a grand exit and disappear into the night, taking the wedding cake with us."

"Steal their wedding cake?" Meryl was horrified.

"Now don't start whining again," Leaflighter warned. "It's not a proper joke if we don't make off with something while they're not looking. Besides, you two need the food, if I'm not mistaken."

Meryl's stomach growled in response. "It just seems a bit much to take the cake, that's all. Why not a leg of mutton?"

"Because she's a fairy," Halstatt answered grimly. "They like to do things with flair. It's what comes of being flighty, indeed, indeed."

And with that, they set off towards the village.

CHAPTER ELEVEN

THEY APPROACHED the village hall with stealth. It looked as though it had been recently built in a clearing that was bordered on one side by the main road and on the other by the forest. Small as it was, it stood as a sign of the tiny village's hopes for growth and prosperity. Fiddle music, laughter and light poured from its doorway and windows. Apparently the entire town had shown up for the festivities. Leaflighter was giggling and beside herself with excitement.

"If you keep laughing like that they'll never believe us," Meryl warned. "I'm sure it isn't godlike to walk about chortling."

"I'll be fine once I'm there." The fairy gestured to them to draw close to her. "We'll wait outside until the bride's father calls for the blessing upon the couple. Usually they just receive a shower of rose petals, but we'll give them something more — the ancient gods themselves come to bless the marriage. They'll love it. Then, while they're all down on their knees adoring us, we'll snatch the cake and run off. Just make sure to run divinely. We don't want them to discover the joke too quickly."

"Run divinely, now, is it? Pine-cones and polliwogs, just how do you suggest we do that? If my mother saw me now she'd drop all her leaves in horror, that she would. It's what comes of adventuring, you see," the draoi said fiercely.

"No doubt," Leaflighter responded cheerfully. "Now, when I signal, we'll step into the doorway, you two on either side of me. Remember, I'll do all the talking. Just look noble and remote."

The three crept to the side of the hall and peeked through a window to watch the dancing. A few times they had to creep back into the shadows when someone came to the doorway for a breath of fresh air. Soon, however, they heard a man's voice shouting down the musicians. Leaflighter hissed, "Start moving nearer now — quietly."

"Well, it's been a wonderful party so far, hasn't it folks?" the voice cried out. Cheers of agreement followed. "And for most of us it's not over yet." More cheers were heard. "But for the lovely bride and her good-for-nothing groom—"

There was laughter and a protesting, "Now, Daddy ..."

"— For them it's time to call an end to this part of the festivities and be off to find a merriment of their own." Great guffaws of laughter. "So let's shower them with our blessings and let them go."

Leaflighter nodded her head and stepped into the doorway. A muffled bang was heard, and the trio were surrounded with a cloud of blue-tinted smoke. Meryl fought back a cough. "You should have warned us about that part," she hissed.

All heads in the room spun to face them. All jaws dropped open at what they saw. A few squeals of fear were heard.

"Greetings," said Leaflighter. Her voice was deep and stern. "Our blessing has been called for and we have come to give it."

There was a momentous pause. Finally one brazen voice piped, "And who the blazes are you ... ma'am?" he added, at the sight of Leaflighter's expression.

"Have the old ways been so long abandoned that we are no longer known?" Leaflighter thundered. Meryl was sure she was having the time of her life. "The time was, mortal, when every earth-being quaked at the sound of my name."

"And ... and that name is, your serene largeness?" quavered another.

Leaflighter drew herself up even taller. She looked at least seven feet tall and the torches cast strange, ominous shadows across her face.

"I am Danu," she declared. "And with me are Branwen and Amaethon. Is our blessing truly asked for, or shall we leave you with a curse?" Her face was a vision of fury.

More shrieks were heard, and people began to fall to their knees.

Meryl felt distinctly uncomfortable. "A bard should be trustworthy," she thought to herself. "I shouldn't be making innocent people look foolish. I'm not a fairy, after all." But she felt herself under Leaflighter's influence and knew that her scruples had come too late.

"Your blessing, your blessing, Great Mother!" was the cry that went up. Leaflighter allowed Danu's features to soften slightly. "Very well," she said, crossing to where the couple stood. Meryl and Halstatt kept close behind her. The mabinog was afraid that she'd trip on her dress, and she was sure that gods didn't trip over their own clothing.

Leaflighter put her hands on the heads of the bride and groom. They were young, both of them dark-haired and no more than eighteen. They looked terrified. Meryl felt her sense of guilt increase. "We give you our great blessing of life and health," the fairy intoned. Then she stepped aside and nodded to Meryl.

The mabinog stepped towards the couple, offering up a mute plea for forgiveness to whatever powers that be. "I give you the blessing of love," she heard herself say. Her voice was surprisingly calm and deep. "More fairy magic," she thought.

She stepped aside and nodded to Halstatt, who positively glared at her as he took her place. Fortunately, all the bowed heads meant that no one but the fairy and Meryl saw it. "I give you the blessing of fertility," he rumbled. Meryl was sure that it took all of Leaflighter's strength to keep his voice from sounding sour.

"Our blessing is given," the fairy said. A shower of rose petals fell from the air upon the crowd. There were so many of them that Meryl's vision was obscured.

"Get to the door," the fairy's voice hissed in her ear. Meryl grabbed Halstatt's arm and tried to run divinely to the doorway without falling over any prostrate forms or dropping the cake that Leaflighter had shoved into her arms.

"Well, wasn't that a lovely show," came a cracked voice. The trio halted. A short, humpbacked figure blocked the door and their route of escape. As the petals cleared they could see an old woman smiling at them wickedly. Her eyes gleamed greenly and there was a gaping hole in her mouth where a front tooth should have been. Her grey hair stood madly on end all about her head, and she was clothed in a patched grey-and-brown dress. She was a true hag. Meryl thought she looked more impressive than the trio did in all their false finery.

"Make way!" Leaflighter bellowed.

The old woman simply smiled more broadly and said, "Ah now, no more tricks then, dearie mine."

Confusion began to stir among the crowd. Many rose from their knees and stared around them at the rose petals that had now drifted down and covered the floor. Meryl was suddenly conscious of her vulnerable situation; it wasn't very godly to be caught holding a stolen wedding cake. She hid herself and the cake behind Leaflighter's cloak.

The villagers recognized the woman in the doorway. "It's mad old Pali Rhys," people began exclaiming. One man stepped forward to try to draw her away. "Come, Pali, you'll not be wanting the gods to curse ye now, will ye?"

The old woman brushed him away. "It's no godly curses I'll be fearing here," she answered.

"What woman is this who dares block our process?" Leaflighter demanded. Meryl thought she heard a note of worry in the fairy's voice.

"It be only old Pali," the helpful man said, trying once again to pull her away. "She be a mite cracked, ye see," he offered by way of an apology.

"Yes, just old Pali Rhys," the hag cackled. "Though folks as know me well call me the fairy's midwife, so they do." She looked triumphantly at the trio.

After that, everything seemed to happen at once. The theft of the wedding cake was noticed, causing a great uproar from the bride and her family. Leaflighter spat into the old woman's eyes. Old Pali began shouting, "It's fairies, me dears! It's all a fairy's trick!" Meryl was horrified to see that the magical disguises had fallen from the trio.

"Run!" Halstatt bellowed, in a most ungodly and undignified manner. The three shouldered past the screaming woman, shaking off the hands that clutched them.

The cry "After them!" went up, and the entire hall emptied itself in pursuit of the three former divinities. Meryl was forced to fling the wedding cake into the face of a man who got too close for comfort.

"To the woods!" Leaflighter called. Even in her terror Meryl could have sworn she was laughing. Then the fairy staggered, almost falling.

"Catch her," Meryl yelped. Together the pair ran with Leaflighter into the forest, Halstatt fending off some pursuers with Meryl's staff.

The three staggered blindly through the undergrowth until the sound of the chase fell off behind them. "I think we've gotten rid of them," Meryl gasped. They collapsed onto the ground and fought for breath.

Halstatt was the first to speak. "Just a little fairy fun," he said sarcastically. "Just dress up like divinities and barrel into a wedding celebration, all for the jolly lark of it," he fumed. "Just pretend that you're a rootless fairy with no consideration in the world and risk having your head beaten in by a herd of enraged humans. Oh my roots and berries, why did I leave my moss patch?"

"Halstatt, be quiet," Meryl snapped. "I think Leaflighter's hurt."

Hurt she certainly was. She was drawn into a ball and shivering. "Get it out, get it out," she begged.

"Get what out? Where?" Meryl searched her desperately for a wound.

"Here it is," the draoi said. He pointed to the fairy's left side, his face sombre. A small arrow was embedded in her flesh. "It's a fairy dart."

"I thought fairy darts made people fall in love, or asleep," Meryl said, puzzled.

"Ah, yes, another fine example of a Hall education, indeed, indeed. Not that kind of dart. It's iron-tipped. If we don't get it out of her she'll turn to cobwebs and blow away."

"Oh dear," Meryl sobbed. She held the fairy's face between her hands. "Leaflighter, I'm going to have to tear it out. It's going to hurt. Try not to scream, okay? They might still be looking for us in the forest."

The fairy nodded. "Just get it out," she said weakly.

It was horrible. Meryl had to grab the arrow's shaft and wrench it from the fairy's side. When it was over, the fairy fainted, and the mabinog did likewise. Halstatt had his hands full, trying to both staunch the blood from the fairy's wound and revive Meryl.

"Sorry," Meryl muttered when she came to. Leaflighter was still unconscious, lying in a curled ball between the roots of a tree. Her face was ashen and her forehead burned to the touch. "Halstatt, what do we do? Can you find the Way and get us back on it?"

Halstatt looked grim and shook his head. "It knows us now. Even if we find it, it won't let us back until Leaflighter tells it to, indeed, indeed it won't. Nor does it look like our fairy friend will be able to do that for a while, if you see what I mean, *hru-umph-nha*."

"But Halstatt, I can't see well enough to look at her wound properly, and we can't light a fire in case the villagers are still looking for us."

The draoi hruumph-nha-ed a fair bit before he responded. "We'll have to find a fairy doctor."

"Is that a fairy who doctors fairies, or a fairy who doctors humans, or a human who doctors fairies?"

Halstatt muttered a few weary expletives about the Hall. "It's a human who has special healing gifts," he explained tiredly. "Gifts passed down through the bloodline of the Meddygon Meddfai."

"The what? And don't start on about the Hall, we haven't time," she added hastily.

"They were the sons of a mortal man and a lake fairy. It's one of your typical human tales — a man captures a fairy wife and is allowed to keep her, with the one stipulation that if he ever touches her by chance with anything of iron she'll disappear. Naturally, being human, he does just that, though to be fair it's usually by accident, indeed, indeed. At any rate, one particular fairy felt badly about deserting her sons, so to them and to their children she gave wonderful healing powers. They're called the Meddygon Meddfai, and the Hall would do well to remember it, *hruumph-nha*."

"So how do we go about finding one of those before Leaflighter turns to cobwebs on us?"

"I'll have to put down roots," the draoi said. "Only a few, down by an old tree. The tree will tell me what it knows. You can always trust a tree, if you see what I mean."

"How long will it take, Halstatt?" Meryl asked anxiously. The fairy moaned beside her.

"I'll start at once," he said, moving off to be near an ancient oak. "Keep her warm."

Meryl searched about in her pouch until she located the dried yarrow leaves that Derwena had packed for her. "In humans these are supposed to stop bleeding," she muttered. "I hope they'll help fairies in the same way." She carefully placed them on the fairy's wound, wrapped Leaflighter as best she could in her cloak and waited through the night.

CHAPTER TWELVE

W HEN DAWN BROKE, Meryl awoke from a troubled sleep. Leaflighter was resting fitfully next to her. Meryl checked her fever and stroked her damp hair, then went to see Halstatt. He was buried in soil up to his waist.

"How is it going?" she asked.

"Fine, fine. I should be able to talk to him soon." The draoi sounded tired.

"Do you want company?"

"I'd be grateful. How's our fairy friend?" He sounded honestly concerned, and not a bit angry. Meryl considered briefly that the draoi was a truly fine fellow.

"She's sleeping, I think. But her forehead's warm. I suppose fairies get feverish too."

Halstatt grunted in response.

"Halstatt, what happened last night? How did that woman know about Leaflighter?"

"Didn't you hear?" he asked impatiently. "She was a fairy midwife. She once helped with a fairy birth, no doubt, no doubt indeed."

"I don't understand."

"Of course not, you never do. The Twlwyth Teg get human women to help with their fairy births. They're always warned that under no conditions should they touch their own eyes while they're going about their business. Naturally, being humans, with a memory equal to that of most butterflies, the women often forget and rub their itchy eye with a finger covered in fairy ointment. They can see fairies, and see through fairy magic, after that.

That is, until some fairy learns of it and stops it, *hruumph-nha*."

"So that's why Leaflighter spat in her eyes?"

"That was fortunate for the woman, indeed, indeed it was. Usually the fairy solves the problem by poking out the woman's eyes, if you see what I mean."

Meryl grimaced. "How unpleasant."

"Yes, well, there you have it. The woman was the one who threw the fairy dart. She'd been waiting for a chance to take her revenge, *hruumph-nha*."

"But why could she still see Leaflighter after that?"

"We could all see Leaflighter, now, couldn't we? I suppose she was staying visible so that you and I could follow her, indeed, indeed I do."

"Oh," said Meryl. She felt forlorn. "Do you think I'm cursed, Halstatt?"

"Eh? How's that?"

"Bad luck seems to follow wherever I go."

"Well, now, I'm sure it wasn't you who insisted we deck ourselves in divine apparel and go frolicking at a wedding dance, if you see what I mean, *hruumph-nha*."

Meryl considered this. "I should have said no," she replied.

"In point of fact, you did say no, didn't you? She refused to listen. Leaflighter's injury is the result of her own actions, indeed, indeed. Just be thankful you weren't hurt in a like manner."

Meryl tried to be comforted by this, but found that she wasn't. Where was the virtue in saying no to something if you went ahead and did it anyway? Before she could think this idea through any further, her stomach rumbled loudly. "I wish I'd kept that cake," she said aloud.

The draoi looked concerned. "You need food, indeed, indeed you do. I'd forgotten you haven't eaten since yesterday's breakfast.

I've had such a nice drink myself with my new roots. Selfish, selfish of me. I do beg your pardon. You'd better wander off and see what you can find to eat."

"Good idea."

Meryl sought out the edible roots and berries she had come to know so well. Fortunately, she found plenty of both — enough to have a good meal and bring some back for later. She wasn't sure if fairies ate roots. "Halstatt will know," she told herself. "I should have asked him earlier."

When she returned, she found Halstatt with an intent look of concentration on his face. She decided not to disturb him and went straight to Leaflighter. Her condition had worsened. She was extremely hot, and she was muttering strange words under her breath. Meryl drew aside the cloak and examined the wound. It was red and angry, and the flesh surrounding it was an ugly greyish colour. Meryl fought a wave of nausea, covered the fairy once more and hurried back to the draoi.

"Halstatt ...?" she said tentatively. "Halstatt, are you almost ready? Leaflighter doesn't look very well."

He lifted an exhausted face to respond. "There's a fairy doctor two days north from here. An old woman named Tanwen Jones. She'll be able to help us." The strain of speaking seemed to weaken him further. His head sank tiredly upon his chest.

Meryl dropped next to him. "Halstatt, don't you dare get sick, too. What's the matter?"

"The matter is I've grown roots in a day that properly should have taken a month to develop, if you see what I mean. I just need to rest a while, and then we can be on our way, *hruumph-nha*." His words ended in a snore.

"Terrific." Meryl sighed and went back to check on Leaflighter. The fairy was obviously in great distress. "She can't wait," the mabinog muttered.

She went back to the draoi and shook him roughly awake. It took some doing.

"Listen, Halstatt. Leaflighter's too sick to wait for you. You stay here and rest while I bring her to Tanwen Jones. When she's better, we'll come back and get you. All right, Halstatt?"

The draoi struggled for a moment, then sank back. "I think that's best," he slurred.

"Does this Tanwen live in a village?"

Halstatt waited before answering. Meryl assumed he was talking to the tree. "No, she lives alone, though there is a village close by. The oak isn't sure of its name."

"So I'll just head north and try to find her," Meryl said resolutely. She felt desperate.

"Just a minute." Halstatt talked to the tree again. "The trees will get the woodpeckers to help you."

"Excuse me?"

"Listen carefully," the draoi gasped. He was obviously fighting unconsciousness. "The trees will tell the woodpeckers to guide you. Follow them." His head dropped again, and he slept.

"All right," Meryl said to the tree. "Send on your woodpeckers. Leaflighter's counting on you."

It was a terrible struggle. At best Leaflighter was only semiconscious, and then she was delirious. Meryl had to carry her in her arms, like a baby, the entire time. Though the fairy was ridiculously light, she was still a heavier burden than the mabinog was used to bearing. Several times Meryl considered leaving her staff, which she wore strapped to her back, and once thought of dropping her harp. She did neither, however. "I'd hate myself for losing them," she told herself grimly. "No matter how awkward they are now."

Hours, then days passed in a strange dream-like way for the young girl. The ravings of the fairy punctuated long, tedious stretches of laborious walking. Meryl stopped rarely, pausing only to eat the last of the roots she'd gathered. And in the midst of it all were the woodpeckers. When one left another would appear, flying in short hops between the trees and guiding Meryl along with cheerful calls. They were faithful, flying into the evening when their sight was failing and all their instincts told them to stop. Meryl was careful to thank each one as she left it on the edge of its territory. And she remembered to ask them to send news to Halstatt that she and Leaflighter were okay.

﹡

Tanwen Jones was in her herb patch watering the plants. Her long, soft brown hair was heavily streaked with grey, and her intelligent face was etched with fine lines, yet she moved briskly among the plants, talking to them and touching them as though they were old friends. She was busy complimenting the rosemary on its scent when a woodpecker landed at her feet and began chirrupping loudly and excitedly. A moment later an exhausted, dirt-stained girl staggered out of the forest, bearing what looked like an unconscious child in her arms.

"Tanwen Jones?" the girl croaked.

"Yes, why yes, child. Come away in before you fall."

The girl turned to the woodpecker. "Can you stay and let Halstatt know how things are?" The bird chirrupped loudly in reply and flew to the windowsill.

Tanwen's eyebrows rose in surprise. She had thought that life held little in it to amaze her anymore, but she had just been proven wrong.

"Come away in," she repeated.

Meryl followed her into the snug dwelling, babbling through her fatigue. "It's true you're a fairy doctor, isn't it? The oak said you were, and Halstatt said you can trust the trees. He's a draoi, so he should know since he's practically a tree himself, though he'd be furious to hear me say that. Can you help her, Leaflighter, I mean, do you think?"

She laid the fairy down on the bed the doctor indicated, close enough to the hearth for warmth, yet beneath a window providing fresh air and light. The floors of the cottage were oak boards, strewn with sweet-smelling rushes, and the stone walls had been whitewashed. It was a place of cleanliness and comfort.

Tanwen Jones drew in a sharp breath when she saw the true identity of the "child" the girl had brought her. She gave Meryl a piercing look. "What has happened here?"

"Well, it was a joke," Meryl began to say, and then she realized what the woman meant. "She was hit by a fairy dart, here, in her side. It was iron."

The doctor's face grew severe when she looked at the wound. "This is very bad," she said. "I will need help. Can you do it?" She gazed doubtfully at the exhausted girl.

"Of course," Meryl replied, straightening herself.

"Good. You must boil a full kettle of hot water. The well's out behind. Go now."

The girl left, and Tanwen turned her attention back to the fairy. The wound looked angrier than ever. The flesh surrounding it was iron-black like the weapon that had done the injury. "Fair one, you've brought me a battle," she muttered to her patient.

Meryl returned with the full kettle and stirred up the fire to bring the water to a boil.

"How's your stomach?" the doctor asked her.

"Empty," Meryl answered, with a wan smile.

"Just as well, there's less chance you'll be sick on me then." Tanwen hurried off to a room divided from the main part by a curtained doorway. "I'll need your help in here," she called out.

Even though she was too tired to think straight, Meryl recognized this as a stillroom, and she gazed in wonder. There were bunches of herbs hanging from the ceiling to dry, bottles full of coloured fluids, a distilling apparatus set up with coils of metal, glass tubes and a burner, and a strange, sweet, musty odour hanging in the air.

Tanwen muttered, poking among the many flasks. She found what she was looking for and shoved it into Meryl's hands. Soon the girl was holding a swath of clean gauze and an evilly sharp, narrow knife.

"Take those things out and set them on the table by the bed. Then come away back," the doctor ordered tersely.

When Meryl returned she found Tanwen crushing something to powder with a mortar and pestle. "What's that?" the girl asked curiously.

"Burnt leather," the doctor replied. She poured it into a bowl and began adding other powders to it. "This is powdered bole, and this," she reached for a distant canister, "this is powdered dragon's blood."

"You killed a dragon?" Meryl gasped.

"Nay!" Tanwen barked a laugh. "Dragon's blood is the name of an herb. Pass me that bottle of spirits." She pointed towards a tall green flask.

"What are you going to do?"

Tanwen paused and looked at the girl levelly. "We've got to get the poison out of her," she said carefully.

"But I took out the arrow."

"Aye, but for a fairy a dart of iron works like an infection in humans. We've got to cut her wound and drain it out. Then the herbs can have a chance to work." Meryl blanched. "Now you can't faint. You must be brave, girl. I've my hands full with the fairy, you understand?" Meryl nodded. "Right. Out we go. That kettle should be boiled by now."

They boiled the thin knife for a moment, then laid it carefully on a bed of clean gauze until it was needed. Meryl held the fairy still while Tanwen washed her wound. The gash was crusted over, but not in a manner that suggested healing.

When she was ready, the doctor took the knife and with a deft cut reopened the fairy's wound, while Meryl struggled to hold Leaflighter down. Tanwen held a basin below the cut, into which poured a mixture of blood and putrid yellow fluid. The sight and smell made Meryl gag, but she resolutely held on to the fairy.

Tanwen pressed about the wound, forcing out all the yellow matter she could. Then she washed the wound out with the hot water and pressed some gauze against it.

"Hold this here. Keep pressure on it," she instructed the girl.

"Now what?"

"Now I make her a dressing to stop the bleeding, and some medicine to fight any poison still in her."

"Will she be all right?"

"Yes, but we must work quickly." The doctor vanished into her stillroom once more, and reappeared after a few moments with some fresh herbs and a flask. "Keep that bandage pressed to her wound," she instructed the girl. "She needs to fight the poison, and this should help." She held the flask to the fairy's mouth and said, "Here now, fair one, drink up," lifting the fairy's head gently as she forced the mixture between Leaflighter's lips. The fairy spluttered a bit but drank it all down. "There," the doctor said. She took a fresh piece of gauze and soaked it in the spirit-and-powder mixture she had made, then added the crushed fresh herbs to the dressing. "This will stop the bleeding cleanly," she said, replacing the original blood-soaked bandage with the new.

"Are you sure she'll be all right?" Meryl asked again.

"We wait now — wait and watch."

"I see," Meryl replied, holding the bandage to Leaflighter's side. She felt the room slowly begin to spin around her and struggled to remain upright.

"In the meantime, you sleep," the doctor said firmly. "There, by the fire. I can't be having you ill as well."

"That's what I told Halstatt," Meryl mumbled groggily. She staggered over to the hearth and lay down on the floor. She was asleep the next instant.

CHAPTER THIRTEEN

W ARM, SWEET LIQUID was gently forced between her lips. Meryl swallowed, opened her eyes and struggled to sit up. The bright brown eyes of a motherly woman looked into her own.

"There, you've had a good sleep. Drink up your tea and come lend a hand with your friend as soon as you can." She touched Meryl's shoulder and then moved away.

In a daze Meryl stared about the cosy room, her memory returning in a rush. "How's Leaflighter?" she demanded, leaping to the bedside where Tanwen Jones now stood.

"Shhh, softly in your speech," the doctor cautioned. "She's sleeping now. Her fever hasn't broken yet, but it's dropped, and she's stopped the raving. I think she'll mend."

"How's her side?" Meryl shuddered, remembering the wound.

"I'm just about to change the dressing. Sit with her until I come back." And she slipped away, leaving Meryl by the sleeping fairy.

"Well, this is what comes of looking for trouble," the mabinog grumbled. "Maybe next time you won't be so stubborn about having your own way. Serves you right — though I'm glad you're not dead," she added hastily.

"An unusual bedside manner," commented Tanwen Jones, on her return. "Just hold this new dressing — and your tongue as well — while I change the old one." Deftly she removed the old bandage and examined the wound. Leaflighter's side was badly bruised but seemed less swollen. Even to Meryl's eyes the cut had a cleaner, healthier look about it. "There now, that's coming along nicely," the doctor whispered. "Hand me that new dressing and then come away."

When the bandaging was done, Meryl had to hold up the fairy's head while Tanwen poured some more strong-smelling medicine down her throat. The girl wrinkled her nose at the concoction. "What's in that, anyway?" she asked.

"Juniper berries to cool the fever, bloodwort to stop any swelling and to keep her sleeping, meadowsweet to dull the pain and garlic to clean the blood and fight infection." The doctor's eyes twinkled at the girl. "It's the garlic that's making you wince, I suspect. People often complain of its smell, but it can't be matched for purifying the blood."

Meryl listened as the fairy's breathing slowed and deepened. "At the Hall we were taught that it's dangerous to mix so many medicines together. We were told that they'd sometimes work against each other and do more harm than good."

The doctor looked at the girl sharply. "And you were taught correctly, as far as humans are concerned," she replied. "But treating one of the fairies is an entirely different matter. Medicines don't mix in their blood the way they do in a mortal's. Each herb works its own healing and doesn't meddle with the others. There's a lesson in there for all of us," she concluded. She made one final check of Leaflighter's pulse and then drew Meryl away with her to a small table on the other side of the room. "Sit yourself down now, and we'll have a proper breakfast."

Proper it was indeed. There were scones, delicately flavoured by sweet herbs, accompanied by fresh raspberry preserves, honey dripping off a piece of comb, clotted cream and piping-hot peppermint tea. Meryl ate until she thought she would burst. When she was finished, she pushed back her chair and sighed contentedly.

The doctor looked at her speculatively, then nodded. "Now you look somewhat more human. A full stomach leads to a clear mind. Perhaps you feel capable of telling me exactly what happened?"

Meryl shifted uncomfortably under Tanwen's level gaze. "Starting from?"

"Starting from how you came to be in the company of a fairy in the first place."

Meryl sighed and settled herself for a long explanation. "You see, I'm a mabinog, and I'm on a quest to become a bard."

Tanwen's eyebrows lifted, but she didn't make any further comment. Encouraged, Meryl went on.

"On my journey I met a draoi, who claimed the bard Taliesin had stolen his magical rosebush from him. We decided to find the rosebush, and the truth, together, so we set off for Avalon."

Tanwen's eyebrows rose higher still.

"Of course, since Avalon's a magical place we decided the best route to get there was on a fairy Way."

The doctor's jaw fell open at this, but still she said nothing.

"Unfortunately, we were captured by fairies on the Way, who were extremely offended by my iron brooch." Meryl pointed to her clasp. "Gwyn ap Nudd agreed to let us try to enter Avalon but insisted that Leaflighter go with us, which is really where all the trouble began," Meryl insisted petulantly. "You see, she insisted on going off the Way to play a practical joke at a wedding festival. Naturally there was a fairy midwife present who saw through the ruse. We ended up running for our lives, and Leaflighter got a fairy dart in her side for her efforts. So Halstatt — my friend the draoi — had to plant himself to learn from the trees where the nearest fairy doctor was, and I followed the woodpeckers to bring Leaflighter to you," she finished triumphantly.

"Well, all in a day's adventures for the average mabinog, I suppose," said Tanwen. There was a pause while she sorted through what she'd been told. "Followed the woodpeckers, you say? There's been one sitting out there in my garden since you arrived."

Meryl leaped up guiltily. "Oh dear, I'd forgotten about him." She ran to the window and whistled. A black-barred woodpecker appeared and landed on the sill. "Thanks for waiting," she said. "Please let Halstatt know that Leaflighter seems to be getting better. If you can check back later, I'll give you more news then."

The woodpecker squawked and flew off. Meryl returned to her seat.

The doctor regarded her steadily across the table. "Do you think you could stand a little peace and quiet for a change? You'll have to wait for your friend to heal."

"Will it take long, do you think?" Meryl asked anxiously. "I really do need to get to Avalon."

Tanwen quirked an eyebrow at the girl's impatience. "Not more than a few days, I shouldn't wonder. Magical beings mend faster than mortals. In the meantime, you could help me about my work. I'd be grateful for a young back to aid me in the garden."

Meryl nodded half-heartedly. "I don't suppose you grow marigolds?"

"Indeed I do," Tanwen said, looking at the girl curiously. "They're useful in the healing of certain wounds. Are you fond of them?"

"Not particularly — just familiar with them, that's all."

"That's champion. If you know about herbs, all the better."

"I only know the basics. My mother loved medicine, and she was always trying to teach me herb lore, but I was more interested in learning new stories. The only herbs I know really well are the ones used in cooking. I had to help with kitchen duties when I lived at the Hall. All the mabinogs did. They said it helped us learn humility."

"And did it?" Tanwen Jones smiled at the girl, and Meryl grinned back.

"No, I don't think so. Humility's a hard lesson for some. I had to embarrass myself publicly before I understood it."

"Nothing teaches like experience," Tanwen replied. "When I was a girl I had to suffer a dreadful case of poison oak before I knew how to properly identify that plant. Now are you ready for some work?" Meryl nodded. "Good. We can't go gathering today — not while our fair friend needs us close by. But the garden is just on the other side of the wall, and I've some weeding that needs doing. That's the best I can offer you in the way of excitement. Come away with me."

Tanwen checked Leaflighter, who was still sleeping soundly, and then led the way out into the garden. It was Meryl's first real look at the place; she had been far too tired and flustered when she had arrived to take any note of it. She stood on the doorstep and gazed about her.

The garden was a magical spot, with an air of peace. Meryl was sure that her mother would have loved it. She could picture her walking about the paths, lost in her thoughts and humming to herself as she used to do when she was happy. The image comforted Meryl, melting away some of the icy pain she felt whenever she thought of her mother. Warmed in her spirit, she looked about at the hawthorn hedge that bordered the garden. There was an opening by a stream in the far left corner where a white willow tree grew. It was through this opening, and not at the gate on the right side, that Meryl had blundered the day before. At the centre of the garden was an elder bush. Meryl remembered kitchen stories of witches living inside elder bushes or trees, and she made a mental note to tread very carefully around Tanwen Jones. Beds of different herbs, some recognizable to Meryl, most not, grew in tidy clusters. There was a network of meandering paths about the garden, providing access to the plants and at the same time keeping the different varieties separated. To the left of the cottage door were some juniper bushes. Meryl looked at them gratefully; they had really helped Leaflighter. And to her right she discovered a rosebush in luxuriant bloom.

"I don't suppose your rose blooms in winter?" she asked the doctor.

"Nay," laughed Tanwen. "Only the witch hazel does that." She pointed to a cluster of bushes on the far side of the roses.

"Really?" Meryl exclaimed. "Is it magical?"

Tanwen laughed again, and a sly look slipped over her face. "Some say so. In the right hands a rod of witch hazel can lead you to water, and it's a champion cure against burns and other afflictions of the skin. But I know people who won't have it near their house — nor the hawthorn or elder neither — for fear it'll bewitch them." She snorted derisively. "Ridiculous notion, of course."

Meryl looked at the doctor's sharp, squirrel-bright eyes and wondered if the idea was so ridiculous after all. Right now, she seemed capable of anything.

"If plants do anything, they help us," Tanwen went on, looking about the garden impishly. "Take these plants over here," she said, directing Meryl to the far side. "This is my poison collection."

Meryl edged a small distance away from her.

"Oh, don't fear; I've never poisoned anyone ... yet. Some people take one look at my foxglove, mandrake, wolfsbane and nightshade and run to the magistrate. They *can* be deadly ... but properly used they are powerful allies against rheumatism, infection, and illnesses of the heart. It's the way of the world," the doctor explained pensively. "Things aren't good or bad of themselves; it's what we choose to do with them that's right or wrong." She shook her head a little and went on. "In fact, I gave your Leaflighter friend some wolfsbane last night to fight off the poison of the iron. You can see for yourself how she fared by it."

Meryl gulped fearfully. "But she hasn't woken up yet, has she?"

Tanwen laughed. "That's the bloodwort. It's well that she's sleeping, for the body mends better when it's resting. Here now," the doctor said, leading Meryl to a small bed of thyme ringed about by marigolds. "This should be less troubling. I haven't been able to weed this for awhile. See what you can do about it." She handed the girl a small metal gardening claw, smiled and moved away.

Meryl dropped to her knees and stared down the marigolds. "Truce?" she asked. Then she began to work.

Her back was sore and the pile of weeds beside her high by the time Tanwen called her to help with Leaflighter.

The fairy was awake and struggling to sit up in bed. Tanwen was firmly holding her down. Leaflighter's cheeks were flushed, but Meryl was relieved to see that the glassy, wild look was gone from her eyes.

"How are you feeling?" she asked, stepping boldly up to the bed.

"I'm fine. Please tell this mortal to let me go," Leaflighter pouted.

"You're better, you mean, not fine. And I'd listen to whatever this mortal says to you — she's the one who saved your life, after all." Meryl found it difficult to keep a sharp tone from creeping into her voice.

The fairy slumped back down and actually seemed to hang her head in shame. "I'm grateful to you," she said mildly. Then her head flew back up, and she laughed merrily. "It was a grand trick while it lasted though, wasn't it?"

"Grand? Grand!? I'll 'grand trick' you!" Meryl shouted.

Leaflighter looked surprised. Tanwen grabbed Meryl and pulled her away from the bed. "You can shriek later, when she's well. Right now she needs rest."

"She looks well enough to me," Meryl muttered. Still, she calmed herself and returned to the bedside. "We've got to change your bandage, Leaflighter, so if you don't want to watch just look out the window."

Tanwen went to get the fresh dressing while Meryl removed the old one. She gasped at the sight of the injury; the bruising was much less and the wound had completely knit itself together.

Leaflighter looked down curiously. "That was rather nasty," she said with surprise. "I wish I had blinded that woman after all. I would have if you hadn't been pulling on me so fiercely," she added crossly.

"You're very welcome," huffed the mabinog.

Tanwen appeared at the bedside again and also exclaimed in pleasure over the healing. "That's champion," she beamed. "I wish my human patients mended so quickly."

"It's one of the advantages of being magical," Leaflighter said smugly. "I should be all better by tomorrow."

"Why wait that long?" Meryl fumed. "We'll just get Tanwen to up your wolfsbane dosage and we'll be out of here by evening."

The fairy paled at that. "Wolfsbane?" she said nervously to the doctor.

Tanwen made some small reassuring noises to the fairy, at the same time throwing Meryl a brief glare. "Now you just drink this down and get some more sleep," she said firmly. "We'll discuss your leaving only after I say so, and not before."

"All right," Leaflighter said, and she yawned. "But I'm only listening to you because it's obvious you're part fairy."

At this Tanwen shook her head and clucked her tongue

reprovingly, but Meryl noticed that the doctor had the impish look in her eyes again. It was clear she was pleased with the observation.

It didn't take very long for the herbs to work. In no time Leaflighter was asleep, and Meryl found herself back out in the garden staring at a new ring of marigolds.

"I went on a quest to avoid you," she said morosely. "It just proves Pedr was right — you can't run away from trouble."

By noon the mabinog was thoroughly tired and a bit dazed by the sunshine. She gratefully answered Tanwen's call to the meal table. There was a jug of cool tea, thick, homemade bread with more honey and a great chunk of cheese, flavoured with herbs.

"Do you even make your own cheese?" she asked, awestruck. It seemed Tanwen could do anything.

"Nay," laughed the doctor. "When I heal someone they pay me in kind. I've no use for coin in my life. What I need I trade for with potions and salves. There's always a need to be met."

Meryl swallowed nervously. "Tanwen, are you a witch? I mean, if you are I assume you're a good one, but do you make magic potions and, well, brews?" she finished lamely.

Tanwen shook her head sadly. "People are always looking for magic," she mused. "Magic is for the fair ones, like your friend there. She can't be spoiled by it, because it's part of who she is. But human people are part of nature and have their own laws to follow. They need time to root, and grow, and blossom, and bear fruit, just like all natural things. Little Nelly Jones was here two days ago, asking for a magic potion to make young Coel fall in love with her. I tried to tell her that love needs to be nurtured with care, not caught in a trap, but she went away sore-spirited and cross. Mortals are always looking for shortcuts. I've never met one who hasn't rued it in the end."

Meryl shifted in her seat. She was sure that the doctor would have a dim view of the magic cauldron. "But what if the shortcut is tried and true?" she argued.

Tanwen gave her a level stare. "Nothing is so true as hard work and patience, though they're rarely the first thing tried, I will admit." She leaned forward and took Meryl's hands, turning their palms up and examining her fingers. "I see calluses here," she said gently. "And though I haven't seen your harp I suspect that they come from playing upon the strings, is that so?" Meryl nodded. "There's no potion that can give you these, though people claim there are some that endow a person with the words of a poet and the voice of a dove. Yet what use is such a voice and such words if your fingers bleed not ten minutes after you've begun to sing? Shortcuts give power without strength. A tree must grow in root as it grows tall; if it doesn't, the first rough wind will blow it down."

Meryl let her hands fall into her lap. "Oh," she said. She looked up at the doctor. "Do you need me for more weeding? Because I'd really like some time to practise; I haven't had much chance lately."

"I think that would be well," Tanwen said.

Meryl fetched her harp from her sack and sat down by the willow tree to play.

CHAPTER FOURTEEN

I T WAS LOVELY TO SIT beneath the willow tree and dangle her feet in the water. Her harp lay next to her, but Meryl didn't pick it up right away. Insead she listened to the melody of the stream. For the first time in days there was nothing she had to do, and she was determined to enjoy it.

It wasn't long, however, before her fingertips began to itch for the harp strings. She picked up the instrument and began to tune it, humming the pitches happily and taking her time with the whole process. Finally she began to pluck out a tune, and she found herself singing the cat song she had written for Pedr. That reminded her of the tree song she had started and never finished, which in turn made her think of Halstatt sitting alone under his oak. "Well, not alone," she corrected herself. "The trees are probably the best company he's had in weeks. No doubt he's as happy as a pig in mud." The thought made her a bit sad, because she found herself actually missing the draoi, ponderous speeches and all.

She went back to her tree song with a determined effort, but nothing seemed to work. Finally she dropped her harp in her lap and glared at the branches of the willow above her. "What's your story?" she demanded of the tree. "How can I write a song if I haven't got a clue what to say?"

"An excellent question," said a voice from behind her.

Meryl leaped up and spun around. "Hello?" she quavered. She was struck with the horrifying thought that she had stumbled upon a second draoi.

"An excellent question," the voice repeated. "Though one can't help but wonder who it was directed towards."

A small man, dressed in mismatched and jumbled colours and sporting a cap with bells and tassels, appeared on the other side of the tree, his eyes twinkling at Meryl. His apparent cheerfulness was the most surprising thing about him, considering that his face above his neat little beard was badly bruised and he seemed to be limping.

"Are you mad?" he asked Meryl. He sounded only curious. "I've heard mad people talk to themselves, though you seem to be rather ordinary in all other respects, if you don't mind my saying so."

Meryl found her voice once again. "Of course I'm not mad. And I wasn't talking to myself, I was talking to this tree." She spoke with as much dignity as she could muster. "I suppose you're here to see Tanwen. I'll tell her you wish to see her, Mr., ah ...?"

"Heini Heilin," he said with a grin, and then a wince as he felt the bruise on his face. "No Mr., just Heini. And I'll go with you. She knows me rather well."

Meryl picked up her harp and led Heini to the cottage. It wasn't until she reached the doorstep that she remembered Leaflighter. She stopped short, turned abruptly to the small man and declared, "Wait here, please," before she dashed into the house, shutting the door on his surprised face as she did so.

Tanwen was in her stillroom, pounding some dried herb with her mortar and pestle and muttering to herself.

"There's someone here," Meryl declared dramatically.

The doctor looked up at her in silence for a moment. "Who?" she finally asked, wiping her hands on the front of an ancient apron she was wearing.

"His name is Heini something-or-other," Meryl said breathlessly. "He says he knows you, but I didn't think, because of Leaflighter and all —" She broke off as Tanwen snorted and brushed past her.

"Well, aren't you a fine sight for aching eyes," the older woman said in greeting to her guest.

Meryl rushed out of the stillroom and stood between the fairy's bed and the door, just to be on the safe side. The small man stood before the doctor, his head bowed penitently, yet from where she was standing Meryl was sure that she could see his eyes twinkling.

"Have you got a new guard dog, Mother?" he said, throwing Meryl a grin. There was no doubt about the twinkle now.

"Mother!" Meryl exclaimed. "Why didn't you tell me? Tanwen, I'm sorry," she said, but Tanwen merely flapped her apology away.

"So," she said sternly, "you've gotten yourself into another fine mess, I see. Come over here and sit by the hearth so that I can examine you properly." Heini hobbled after her and plunked himself down on a stool.

Meryl stole a quick glance at the fairy; she was still sleeping peacefully. The mabinog made a mental note to be careful of taking any sleeping draughts mixed by the doctor.

"It was simply a case of excessive enthusiasm," Heini was explaining between winces as his mother examined his bruised face. "I was having a great romp and causing a grand rollick by imitating Coel as he danced, and I got a bit carried away and —"

"And hit a bit too close to the mark, and earned yourself a royal beating," Tanwen finished for him. Heini grinned his agreement as best he could with his chin pinched firmly in Tanwen's hand. "Always it's the same tale you bring home with your bruises," the doctor sighed. "This is the fifth time in a year, and you still haven't learned moderation."

"And never will, Mother-o!" the small man cried gaily. "Fooling has nothing to do with moderation. That's for Coel's advisers, and a sorry lot they are for it. Now, aren't you going to give me one of your magical brews and a biscuit, and leave off mothering for a time?" He threw Meryl a wink. She grinned in return; one couldn't help feeling cheerful around Heini. Tanwen gave him a soft cuff on his ear and disappeared to her stillroom.

Heini examined Meryl as he waited for his "magical brew." "Well," he said at last, "you're not a visiting lunatic, nor a guard dog. What, if I may make so bold to ask, are you then?"

"I'm a questing mabinog," Meryl said importantly.

"That would explain the harp," he said, "though not the sounds I heard coming out of it. So how is it that you came questing through my mother's cottage? Not after some magical potion to sweeten your voice, I hope, because Mother is rather firm about those matters."

"Of course not," Meryl snapped. She didn't appreciate the slur against her musical abilities, and she suddenly found herself disenchanted with Heini. No doubt his bruises had been well deserved! "I brought a sick friend to her, and I'd thank you to keep your voice down because she's sleeping over there." Meryl gestured to the corner bed.

"I see," Heini replied, "though in point of fact I think it is you who had better keep your voice down."

Meryl was about to reply when a grunt from the bed in question caught her attention. The next moment a rather wild-haired Leaflighter sat up in bed and announced, "I'm starving!"

Tanwen reappeared from the stillroom, glared at the two by the fire and marched over to the bed.

"I really *am* starving," the fairy repeated petulantly.

"That's a grand sign," the doctor said. She called Meryl to her side and gave her a bowl of herbs. "Here, boil some water and steep these in a cup for his nibs over there while I check her dressing."

Leaflighter noticed then that there was someone else in the room. "What is that disreputable mortal doing here?" she demanded.

"I could just as easily ask what a disreputable fairy is doing in my mother's daybed," Heini replied.

Leaflighter glared at him. "Don't bandy words with me, human. I've half a mind to curse you to the ninth generation just for wearing that offensive clothing."

Meryl decided that things had gone far enough. "You can't curse your doctor's son in her own home, Leaflighter. That would hardly be polite. Besides, you're just cranky because you're hungry and you've done nothing but sleep for the past two days."

Tanwen chose to intercede as well. "Your wound is nicely healed — I won't bother with another dressing. But you should stay in bed, and I'll give you some more medicine to fight any lingering infection."

"Medicine doesn't sound very filling," Leaflighter complained.

"You may have some clear soup," Tanwen said. "Nothing more," she added sternly, as the fairy opened her mouth to protest.

Meryl had finished making Heini his tea, which she handed to him in one of Tanwen's heavy clay mugs. "When you said that you came with a sick friend I must admit that I imagined something far tamer," he commented.

"You're welcome," Meryl replied. He looked confused. "For the tea," she explained. He still continued to stare at her blankly. She rolled her eyes and went over to Leaflighter's bedside. Tanwen had disappeared into the stillroom once again.

"I'm glad you're feeling better," she told the fairy. "Hopefully we can be on our way soon."

"Where's the tree-twin?" Leaflighter suddenly demanded.

"He's in the forest. He had to root himself by an oak to get directions to Tanwen's. We'll go back for him when you're well."

"Tree-twin? Rooted?" Heini looked back and forth from fairy to mabinog.

"My friend, Halstatt," Meryl explained. "He's a draoi. We're travelling together to Avalon on a quest."

"I see." The small man studied her in silence. "I see that I've greatly underestimated you," he added after a moment. "A mabinog travelling to Avalon in the company of a draoi and a member of the Twlwyth Teg — yes, I'd have to say that I've truly underestimated you."

Meryl felt strangely proud. The way he spoke made her feel noble and rare. She only hoped that the Queen of Avalon would agree with him.

Tanwen appeared once more and set Meryl scurrying to the well again with the kettle. When she returned she found the fairy and Heini in conversation.

"I'm a professional fool," he was saying. His mother snorted at that, but he continued bravely on. "I work for young Coel, entertaining his court, as he likes to call it."

"Court indeed," Tanwen huffed. "A lot of layabouts with nothing better to do than laugh at some silly fellow and then beat him about the ears when he speaks too true."

"Mother would prefer that I were a physician, as she is," Heini explained with a grin. "But I've never had the trick with my hands that she has, and sickness makes me cross. I prefer the life of the paid silly fellow, as she calls it."

"There's no trick to healing, just a lot of hard work," Tanwen replied.

"Ah well, there's the trouble then, Mother. There's plenty of tricks to what I do, and I wouldn't have it any other way."

"That's the fairy blood in you," Leaflighter said approvingly. She looked pointedly at Meryl.

"Even when you get a broken head?" Meryl asked the fool. She looked pointedly back at the fairy's injury.

"That is the one drawback to the job," Heini conceded,

rubbing his bruised cheek tenderly. "People may say that Coel is a merry old soul, but he does have a heavy fist at the end of his arm for all that."

"I still see no need for that horrible motley outfit you're wearing," Leaflighter interjected. "Was that part of the punishment for having offended this young lord?"

"King, actually," Heini corrected her. Tanwen snorted once again, this time at the title. Meryl had to agree that it was rather ostentatious; most fine folks in Albaine weren't so showy. "Well, he does have a large amount of land," Heini explained patiently. Meryl was sure that the mother and son had discussed this many times before. "But as for my suit, I designed it myself," he said to the fairy. "It adds to the silliness, and it helps me stand out in the crowd at court."

"It's horrible," she replied. "It looks like a mockery of the King's cloak."

Meryl looked at the fool in surprise. Leaflighter was right, actually. Heini was dressed in stockings with one leg of blue, the other of red, with a white jerkin covered in green and yellow diamond-shaped patches. He had a blue shoe on his red leg and a yellow shoe on his blue leg. He had taken off the bizarre three-pronged hat he had been wearing, to allow his mother to examine his bruises. It was a strange cap that slipped over his head like a hood, leaving an opening for his face, and it had three points of red, blue and green that finished in tassels with bells on the ends. It certainly would have made its wearer stand out in a crowd.

"It does," Meryl agreed. "Only the King's cloak doesn't have any yellow in it."

"What are you talking about?" Heini asked in confusion. "Coel doesn't have a cloak anything like this."

"Oh, not King Coel," Meryl replied. "Gwyn ap Nudd, the King of the Fairies."

There was a weighty silence. "Oh," Heini finally replied. He seemed to be at a loss for words.

"Speaking of the King," Meryl said nervously to the fairy, remembering the judgement she was still under, "will we be in any sort of trouble if we wait much longer?"

The fairy frowned, then shook her head. "We should be back on the Way in a few days. We'll leave tomorrow, whatever the good doctor says."

"I heard that," Tanwen replied.

"We've pressing business, you see," Meryl explained. "Leaflighter's so much better — at the rate she's healing she should be right as rain by tomorrow."

"Tomorrow will tell its own tale," the doctor replied firmly. "You can wait until then before you start making any plans. For now, I could use your help in preparing a meal. We'll leave the invalids to themselves."

She gave the fairy another mild dose of herbal tea, and she must have put something similar into the brew she had made for Heini, because before long they were both snoring softly, Heini slumped over in a rocking chair that his mother had drawn near the hearth.

Meryl cut up vegetables and herbs as Tanwen directed. Then she stirred the soup over the fire while the doctor made another batch of her flavoured biscuits. Soon the cottage was filled with a delicious aroma. Meryl found her stomach growling.

Eventually the good smells awakened the patients and the four of them sat down to supper. Despite all of Tanwen's protests Leaflighter joined them at the table. "I can't possibly lie down any longer," she declared. "I've begun to feel like an enchanted princess as it is."

Heini kept them entertained while they ate. Everything was a joke to him, and he often had them laughing till they cried with his stories of life at Coel's court. Meryl wished that the Hall could hear about his antics; the bards would never accuse her of being flighty again. She felt positively sedate in comparison with him.

"So," he said, changing the conversation abruptly, "what sends you to Avalon in the company of a fairy and a draoi?"

Meryl was flustered; she didn't know how to begin to answer that question.

"Oh, she's under trial of the King," Leaflighter responded airily. "She brought iron on our Way, and she has to prove her worth to the Queen to escape punishment." The fairy grinned contentedly at Meryl and ate another biscuit.

"I think I liked it better when you were sick," the mabinog grumbled. Leaflighter only grinned some more, this time with a mouth full of biscuit crumbs.

"Iron on the Way," Heini said. "That was begging for trouble — as though being on the Ways in the first place wasn't bad enough."

"Hindsight is always the sharpest," Tanwen said calmly.

"We were just trying to find the most direct route to Avalon," Meryl insisted. "We didn't mean to offend anyone."

The whole tale then came out in a jumble, with frequent interruptions from Leaflighter. By the end of it Heini was stroking his small pointed beard. His eyes were twinkling so brightly that Meryl was sure they cast a light.

"Mother, I've been thinking ..." he began.

"A most rare and unusual occurrence," she replied waspishly.

"Nay, seriously. I've been thinking that I can't go back to Coel's for another week or so, until his wrath is cooled. Wouldn't it make more sense for me to travel to Avalon with these two than to be sitting about here getting in your way and vexing your work?"

"No, it would not," Tanwen replied.

"Besides, we didn't invite you," Meryl pointed out. She was sure Halstatt would have something to say about Heini's manners.

"Of course you may come!" Leaflighter crowed.

Both Meryl and the doctor turned to glare at the fairy.

"Oh come, he'll be good fun, and not such a stick-in-the-mud as you've been," the fairy said to the mabinog.

"Stick-in-the-mud?! Stick-in-the-mud!?" Meryl bellowed.

"That's right," Leaflighter replied calmly.

Meryl thought about choking the fairy. Fortunately, Tanwen's good sense stopped her.

"Why would you accompany them, son? You've no part in their quest, or in their trial."

"True, but it seems too rare a treat to pass up — the chance to see the Summer Land and walk on the fairy Way. Besides, I might be of some assistance. I'm part fairy, as you've always proudly told me, and I'm accustomed to dealing with royalty."

"Not fairy royalty," Meryl pointed out icily.

"Royalty's royalty," he replied.

"This is a serious quest," Meryl said.

"All the more reason to bring along a fool; it keeps the mood light and puts things in perspective."

"Hear, hear," Leaflighter cheered.

"I don't think Halstatt would like it," Meryl insisted. "He has enough trouble dealing with one human and a flighty fairy. A fool might drive him to insanity. I wouldn't want to be found too near a lunatic draoi."

"That's just it," Leaflighter replied. "That barky-being needs some loosening up. He's too stiff by far."

"I think you should speak more politely about someone who helped save your life," Meryl snapped.

"And I thank him for it!" Leaflighter declared cheerfully.

Heini got down on one knee, took Meryl's hand in his own and stared up at her earnestly. "Please, please, allow me to accompany you and your party to Avalon. It would give me the greatest pleasure, and I promise you that you won't regret having me."

Meryl felt her cheeks grow hot with embarrassment. She pulled her hand away. "Oh, all right," she gasped in confusion.

Leaflighter and Heini began to dance a jig about the room together, the fool bursting into an impromptu song.

Now listen to a story of a forest oracle,
Discovered in the bumblings of a young mortal.
Together they went questing for a magical rose,
Though how they hoped to find it only heaven truly knows.
If it wasn't for a fairy friend, assisted by a fool,
The journey would have come to naught,
        a disappointment cruel.

"I think I already do regret it," Meryl said to Tanwen.

The doctor simply shook her head. Strangely enough, she also smiled.

CHAPTER FIFTEEN

T HE THREE LEFT the next day, Leaflighter being thoroughly cured and completely irrepressible. Tanwen packed them a huge supply of biscuits and other travelling edibles. Meryl remarked that they had food enough to last them all the way to Avalon and back again.

"That's the idea," the doctor replied cheerfully. She appeared to have conquered all her reservations about her son's journey to the Summer Land. Meryl tried to get her to explain why, but she slipped out of the discussion every time with, "You never know what will be good for people."

The mabinog had to admit, however, that the fool and the fairy made merry travelling companions. The first day passed by quickly, filled with laughter and singing at every step. On the second day, however, Meryl couldn't shake a growing and eerie sense of foreboding. She kept insisting that something was wrong and that they needed to hurry. The others tried to jolly her out of this mood, but she tensely rushed the group along.

When at last they arrived at the clearing with the ancient oak tree they found only an empty, gaping hole in the spot where Halstatt had been rooted, with earth flung madly about. Meryl instantly fell into a frenzy.

"Where did he go?!" she shrieked at the tree. The oak remained silent, but four agitated woodpeckers in its branches responded at once, simultaneously.

"Do you know what they're saying?" Meryl asked, clutching Leaflighter by the arm and bellowing the question into her face.

The fairy shook herself free of the terrified mortal and flapped her arms at the birds. "Order, order at once!" she cried. The noise stopped. Then Leaflighter pointed to a small, female woodpecker and said, "You. Tell us what has happened here."

The woodpecker spluttered slightly, and the fairy had to quell several interruptions from the others, but the story soon came out. It appeared that the draoi had been uprooted and kidnapped by a pair of burly, bearded men who swore a great deal. Despite all the efforts of the woodpeckers (here they all interrupted at once to describe the brave deeds they'd performed in the defence of the draoi), the two men had succeeded in tearing Halstatt away.

"Where did they take him?" Meryl bellowed.

"Towards the high road," Leaflighter translated again. "They're willing to take us to the spot."

"Let's go!" Meryl was already storming off in the direction the woodpeckers had indicated.

"Just a moment," Heini called after her.

She stopped and turned impatiently. "Well?"

"Don't you think we'd better have a plan for when we finally overtake these brutes?" he said, sensibly.

"Oh, Leaflighter can just turn us into gods again, or maybe monsters." Meryl's eyes began to glow fiercely. "I'd like to be a horrendous sea monster. They'll be sorry they ever tangled with that particular draoi."

The fool turned to the fairy. "What do you think?"

She was grinning widely. "Sea monsters it is," she replied.

"I have a bad feeling about this," Heini muttered as he followed the other two.

"Can't be as bad as what those kidnappers will be feeling," Meryl snapped back grimly. Leaflighter just laughed, as usual.

The trail would have been obvious, even without the woodpeckers. Clearly Halstatt had not made a gracious victim; there were signs of struggle the entire way. Small branches were snapped off trees, the ground was muddied and pitted with footprints and the gouges made by dragging roots, and there were shreds of brown homespun clothing stuck to various bushes. This made Meryl proud and terrified at the same time; she hoped that the draoi had not got himself seriously hurt. Her fears escalated when the signs of struggle stopped abruptly. She paused and examined the tracks.

"The prints are deeper here, and there's no sign of Halstatt's roots. They must have carried him, and he wouldn't have let them do that if he could have avoided it. If they knocked him out ..." Her voice trailed off. She looked sternly at the fairy. "Make me into the scariest monster you can imagine when we find them."

"Righty-o," the fairy replied, equally grimly. If Meryl hadn't known fairies better, she would have said that Leaflighter was actually concerned about the draoi.

"Be more optimistic," Heini responded. "Maybe he refused to walk another step and forced them to carry him to slow them down."

"I hope so," was all Meryl could reply.

Three pairs of eyes peered through the veil of underbrush and examined the camp. There was a smoking fire pit in the centre of the small clearing, a rough tarp hanging from a bough for shelter, two dark, burly men arguing in hushed tones at the far side and a highly nonplussed draoi sitting, bound and gagged, beneath a nearby tree. The watching eyes glared, then withdrew.

"Okay, turn us into monsters," Meryl hissed. "Heini can untie Halstatt while we scare them into an early grave."

"Not so fast," Leaflighter hissed back. "The lighting is all wrong. We have to wait until dusk or it'll spoil the effect."

"The only effect we need is terror," Meryl snapped. "Now isn't the time to worry about aesthetics."

"I'm with Leaflighter," Heini said, "though not for artistic reasons. If we wait a while and observe them we might get a better idea of what this is all about. That could help us."

"I don't see how," Meryl stormed. She was having trouble keeping her voice to a whisper. "The only thing this is about is saving Halstatt. We can ask questions later."

"Well, I want to wait until the lighting is better," the fairy sniffed. "So you'll just have to be patient and go along with us. Besides, a little spying sounds like fun."

"Fun! Halstatt's a prisoner, and you're talking about fun?"

"There you go being a stick-in-the-mud," Leaflighter said. "Halstatt looks well enough to me."

"I'm sure he'd be delighted to hear that," Meryl fumed.

The others won out in the end. The companions drew near the camp again for further observation. Heini kept insisting that it made the best strategic sense. "You don't need much strategy when you're a monster," Meryl kept grumping. The others told her to hush.

When they returned to their spy post they found that the pair of kidnappers had finished arguing with one another and were now in heated debate with the draoi. Halstatt's gag had been removed, and he was evidently making the most of the situation.

"Your entire scheme is simply preposterous," he was exclaiming. "You clearly are individuals with a sorely limited understanding of draoi, indeed, indeed."

"Ye can so do it!" bellowed the shorter and thinner of the two men. "And ye will do it, too, or we'll pull off more of yer roots!"

Meryl growled, but the draoi looked remarkably calm. "Go ahead," he replied. "They grow back, you know. I'm a regenerative being, unlike you pesky humans, *hruumph-nha.*"

His response seemed to fluster the kidnappers. They withdrew for another heated argument, then returned after a new plan had been decided upon.

"Right," said the smaller man, firmly. "If ye don't tell us when the next rich man is passin' by, we'll set ye on fire."

The draoi blanched at that, though it was unlikely that anyone other than Meryl knew him well enough to notice.

"Look here," he said desperately, "I just am not able to do what you're asking. An oracle is not a fortune-teller. You've gotten your ridiculous human legends confused. What you need is one of those bizarre women who puncture their ears with gleaming metal rings and spend all their spare moments staring into glass orbs. All I can do is give you some sound advice about this year's harvest, or perhaps suggest an alternative career option, if you see what I mean."

"It's lyin'," grunted the taller and more burly of the pair, in a doubtful tone. He scratched his thick rusty curls and looked to his companion for guidance.

"I'm a 'he,' not an 'it,' if you please," Halstatt snapped.

"I can't believe it," Meryl fumed to her companions. "They want to use Halstatt to sniff out potential robbery victims. How could anyone think of such a thing?"

"You have to admit, it is rather ingenious," Heini replied, and Meryl thumped him on the ear.

"There's no point in waiting any longer," the mabinog growled. "Lighting or no lighting, we need to save him now, Leaflighter."

"Oh, all right," the fairy grumbled. "But I'm only agreeing with you because I'm starting to get a cramp. On the count of three I'll transform us. Heini, you free the tree-twin, and we'll terrorize the criminals." She paused for a moment, then grinned in delight. "I've thought of the perfect creatures. Are you ready?" The others nodded. "One ... two ... three!"

The companions leaped out into the clearing, roaring fearfully. In horror the abductors and the hostage stared at two hideous, gargantuan, slime-mouthed beasts rearing like watery dragons in their midst. It took a moment for Meryl to realize that she was shrieking like a banshee but was otherwise still her everyday self. She stopped short. The two monsters halted their roaring and stared at her as well.

"Oh dear," said the larger monster, "I forgot about that iron brooch of yours again."

"Don't just stand there, roar!" Meryl bellowed. "I'll free Halstatt."

"Look here," said one of the confused criminals, "what's going on?"

"You're about to be eaten," Meryl snapped. "Run away properly."

The draoi, meanwhile, had recovered from his initial shock. "My dear girl!" he cried. Then he regained his dignity and muttered, "And high time it is, too. You've been a painfully long time about this rescue, even for a flighty human being, indeed, indeed."

"Ye know this person?" the smaller and slightly bald kidnapper asked the draoi. Halstatt's reply was cut off by Heini's roar. The criminals cowered. Meryl began to untie her friend, which emboldened the kidnappers.

"Here, that's our oracle!" the larger one yelled.

"He was mine first. You stole him!" Meryl yelled back.

"He was just sittin' in the forest. We found him fair and square."

"Well, I left him there and was coming back for him," Meryl bellowed over the clamour of the monsters.

"Finders is keepers!" shrieked the smaller criminal in response.

"Would you all kindly be silent!" howled the draoi. Even the monsters stopped and blinked at him. "May I remind you all," he continued icily, "that I am nobody's draoi but my own." He shook off the remaining ropes, and Meryl's possessive hands into the bargain. He glared fiercely at the larger monster. "You look perfectly ridiculous," he said. "Resume your proper form, such as it is, at once."

The monster pouted, but did as it was bid. In a twinkling Leaflighter was before them, grinning impishly.

The draoi turned his gaze upon the other monster. "Am I to assume, then, that this is his natural guise?"

"That depends," said Meryl stonily.

"On what, if I may be so bold to ask?"

"On whether or not these kidnappers are willing to let you go."

"If they don't I'll just curse them," Leaflighter answered cheerfully. The monster abruptly became Heini again. The kidnappers looked increasingly dazed.

"Heini Heilin, king's fool, at your service," he said graciously to Halstatt, sweeping him a formal bow.

"What an appalling costume," the draoi replied.

"You needn't be rude. He has helped rescue you, after all," said Meryl.

"The bark-brain is just grumpy because he missed out on being a monster," Leaflighter proclaimed.

The smaller of the criminals chimed in before Halstatt could reply. "Would somebody please tell me what in the blazes is goin' on here? And just what kind of creature be she?" he added, pointing at Leaflighter.

"I don't think we owe you any sort of explanation in the

least," Meryl snapped, turning furiously upon the kidnapper. "Anyone who goes about abducting innocent oracles for the purposes of highway robbery is beneath consideration, so there." She turned back to Halstatt and asked, "Are you ready to go?"

The larger of the two thieves began to snivel. "We never wanted to be robbers," he wept.

The smaller of the two shuffled his feet and said, "Buck up, now, Orwig."

"No, I won't buck up," the larger fellow replied. "I want to go back to bein' an honest scarecrow, I do, and not have any more truck wi' monsters nor oracles." He began to sob tragically into a large red handkerchief.

The other robber thumped him on the back and glared at the puzzled companions. "I hope ye're all pleased wi' yournselves," he growled. "Ye've upset my brother here somethin' terrible."

"Upset your brother!" Meryl replied hotly. "You're the crooked ones here, not us!"

"Oh, easy to say, easy to say, I'm sure, when ye haven't lost the only job yer family's ever done, and been turned out of the village what yer own great-great-grandmother founded. Easy to point the finger then at a pair of lorn brothers just tryin' to survive as best they may."

"Well, I'm sure that's all very difficult," Meryl said, "but it still doesn't excuse what you did to my friend here."

"Oh, if I were only back in the field, wi' the corn growin' greenly around me!" the larger brother wailed. Heini offered him another handkerchief, as the red one was completely drenched.

"Suppose we all have a seat by the fire and you tell us about it," the fool suggested kindly.

Meryl was thunderstruck. "A seat by the fire? Together? Heini, have you gone completely mad? These people kidnapped Halstatt, for goodness sake!"

"I think that would be a highly appropriate way of resolving this conflict, I do, indeed," Halstatt interjected. He settled himself at what he thought was a safe distance from the fire and was joined by everyone except the mabinog. She stared at the group in perplexed rage. Leaflighter was cheerfully handing Tanwen's biscuits around the circle.

"You are all lunatics," Meryl stated calmly. "Absolute lunatics."

"And you," the fairy said gleefully through a mouthful of biscuit, "are being a stick-in-the-mud again. Come sit down and have something to eat."

Meryl was given a biscuit and introduced to Irwyn, the smaller robber who was also the elder brother, and Orwig, who had dried his tears and was now munching contentedly on a piece of cheese.

"We was professional scarecrows," Irwyn was explaining, "just as all our ancestors had been. We was the best in the business. Together we had a two-acre field to patrol, and never a crow was seen near our corn."

"That's a large bit of land," Heini said.

"Aye, and it made the other scarecrows sore jealous," Orwig replied.

"That it did, brother," Irwyn answered. "So jealous that they conspired against us."

"You don't say," Leaflighter breathed. She looked as though she was thoroughly enjoying herself, as indeed she was.

"Oh aye. They slipped somethin' into our noon ale to make us sleep, one day. And sleep we did, right out in the master's fields, for he'd have none but my brother and myself patrol his corn."

"It was all eaten," Orwig said, beginning to sob again. This time it was Leaflighter who gave him a handkerchief.

"We didn't wake till sundown, when the crows had picked every stalk clean," Irwyn finished. He bitterly kicked another log onto the fire.

"But surely you could plead your case," the draoi said. "Even a human judge would have to agree that you were framed, *hru-umph-nha*."

"We never went before any judge," Irwyn replied. "The master's crop was gone and the sleep still hung heavy in our eyes. We thought we was guilty ourselves. It weren't till later, when we was disgraced and forced to leave our homes, that we started to see things clearly."

"What do you mean?" Heini asked.

"Well, it were common for us to eat our noon meal in the fields, our sister Mary bringin' us our food and a fresh pint each from the inn. But this day it were a local lad as brought it to us, sayin' as how Mary were kept busy at home wi' a sick cow. We thanked the lad and thought nothin' of it, but we wondered a bit, as we knew 'im as the son o' one of the other scarecrows what has had 'is eye on the master's land for many a year now."

"So, you drank the ale and promptly fell asleep," said Heini.

"Aye," Irwyn replied. He began to sniff once more.

"Have you never fallen asleep in the field before?" Halstatt asked suspiciously. "Never dozed off in the warm noontime sun, if you see what I mean?"

"Never," snapped Orwig indignantly. "We're professional scarecrows, like we's said, and know how to mind corn. We hardly even sit still to eat, always movin' about we is, keepin' the crows away from the crop."

"Even if you were tricked, couldn't you simply get jobs as scarecrows in another village?" Meryl asked, caught up in the story in spite of herself.

"Scarecrowin's a family business," Irwyn explained patiently. "Ye can't just step into the job. It has to be passed on."

"So you decided to become robbers instead."

"Well, we was wanderin' in the forest, bemoanin' our outcast state, when we stumbled upon this oracle asleep under the tree. Granny had taught us about them, and we could hardly believe our luck when we found one. We'd become desperate men, you see," Irwyn said to the draoi. He nodded sympathetically; Meryl could hardly believe her eyes. "We thought we could use him — beggin' yer pardon — to track down rich folks on the high road what we could steal from, just till we got back on our feet. We only planned to rob the mean, miserly ones as could afford it," he added in his own defence.

"I think that's highly creditable of you," Heini said.

"Well, I don't," Meryl snapped. "Robbery's robbery. You could have just asked Halstatt for some helpful advice. He's very good about that."

"Thank you," said the draoi, looking at Meryl with pleasure.

"We see that now," said Orwig. "But like my brother was sayin', we was desperate men." He seemed to like the sound of that phrase, for he repeated it lovingly. "Desperate, desperate men, that's what we was."

"And is your home village far from here?" asked Heini.

"Two days east," Irwig answered sadly. "We hadn't the heart to roam very far, you see, not knowin' anythin' of the wide world."

"Well," said Heini, "it's a clear case of injustice, there's little doubt of that. The only thing to do is to bring these unfortunate men back to their village and help them argue their case before a proper judge."

Meryl spluttered, horrified. "We can't do that, Heini!" she declared. "We have to get back on the Way to Avalon before the King notices we've been gone."

The draoi's head snapped up at that. "We?" he said, looking pointedly at Heini. "What do you mean by 'we,' if you don't mind my asking, *hruumph-nha?*"

"Oh, I don't mind at all," Heini replied merrily. "I'm going with you to Avalon — they've invited me."

Halstatt turned a baleful glare upon Meryl. "Is this so? You've invited this highly unorthodox human creature to accompany us on our sacred quest, upon which our freedom — our very lives, in fact — depends? This is so?"

"Well —" began Meryl.

"Yes," said Leaflighter.

"Do ye mean the magical Avalon?" Orwig interrupted. "The Summer Land where dreams come true?"

"Yes," said Leaflighter again, her smile splitting her face nearly in two.

"But it can wait," Heini said grandly. "The most important thing is that you have your profession and your reputations restored. Drawing on my elocutionary skills, the wisdom of this honourable draoi, the magic of this fairy and the, ah, more intangible qualities of this mabinog —"

"Thanks a lot!" snapped Meryl.

"— we shall earn you back your places in your master's fields and favour before the next phase of the moon," he finished, with a bold sweep of his arm.

The draoi began to rant, Meryl began to argue, the brothers began to cheer, Heini began to munch another biscuit, and Leaflighter began to laugh. It took a while for the noise to sort itself out.

At the end of the day, at dusk's idyllic hour when the twilight is perfect for performing magical tricks, it was decided that a party of six would be wending its way to the scarecrows' village in the morning.

Meryl never could remember why she'd agreed to the idea.

CHAPTER SIXTEEN

IT WAS A FANTASTIC GROUP that set out at daybreak. The scarecrows and the fool walked together, discussing the many similar requirements of their professions: namely, the possession of a loud voice and the necessity of dressing to be noticed. Leaflighter skipped about on her own, often vanishing altogether and then leaping back into sight unexpectedly. Halstatt and Meryl walked behind the others.

"My quest has been hijacked," Meryl complained bitterly.

"Snakes and snowdrops, you're the one who invited the fool along," Halstatt grumped in return.

There wasn't much Meryl could say to that, so she wisely kept her mouth shut. Her melancholy was contagious, however, and in a few moments Halstatt spoke again, mournfully.

"This is what comes of leaving one's moss patch. If I were a proper draoi I'd be sitting there now, quietly reflecting on a new riddle, indeed, indeed I would."

Meryl was taken aback. "What do you mean, a 'proper draoi'? Of course you're a proper draoi. The only riddle you need to solve is the mystery of your rose, and you can't do that sitting in a moss patch."

"*Hruumph-nha,*" was his only response.

"Besides," Meryl added, doing her best to sound cheerful, "I've never gone before a judge before. Maybe it'll be good practice."

"Practice?"

"You know, for pleading our cause to the Queen."

"Ah yes, in the midst of our present misery, I'd almost forgotten our impending doom, *hruumph-nha.*"

"It doesn't have to be our doom," Meryl said earnestly. "Don't you think things happen for a reason, Halstatt? Maybe we can learn something from this that will help us win our way to Avalon."

"Or perhaps we'll win our way further into the wrath of the fairy King and end up cursed and bald the minute we set our feet back on the Way."

"Fate couldn't be so unkind. Not after all we've gone through."

"Fate could indeed be so unkind. I know thousands of instances from history in which Fate has been exactly that, and seemed to take some sort of ghoulish delight in it as well, *hruumph-nha.* You might easily say that it's the one thing you can count on when you're dealing with Fate, indeed, indeed."

"Oh dear. Well, since we can't help it, I guess we should just hope for the best," Meryl answered gloomily.

"Typical human response to adversity." Halstatt sniffed. "If you don't like something, then you simply refuse to think of it and expect that will make it go away, indeed, indeed you do."

They might have quarrelled then if Leaflighter had not picked that moment to come hurtling down from the branches above them. They both shrieked at the fairy instead, which brought the fool and the scarecrows back to see what all the ruckus was about. Once the dust had settled, the decision was made almost unanimously that it was time for a break and a snack. Halstatt muttered a few objections and dropped ominous reminders of impending curses, but the fairy hushed him with a well-timed "Shut-up, stodge-stalk." It left the poor draoi incensed beyond speech, which was exactly what Leaflighter had intended.

"What are we going to say to this judge?" Meryl asked as she munched on a handful of berries.

"Oh, I'll think of something — public speaking is my gift," Heini responded cheerfully.

"I was hoping for a more specific answer," Meryl shot back

dryly. "We can hardly just walk into some local magistrate's office and demand to be heard."

"And why not?" demanded Leaflighter.

"Because we look like a troupe of wandering lunatics, that's why," Halstatt croaked, finding command of his voice again, if not his temper. "We'll be run out of town before we get the chance to say a word, *hruumph-nha*."

"Who is the judge in your village, anyway?" Meryl asked quickly, hoping to turn the discussion in a different direction.

Irwyn sighed. "He's a fearsome man indeed is old Jack Williams. He's eighty-five years old if he's a day, and he's been the village's judge for as long as most folks can remember."

"Eighty-five!" exclaimed Meryl. "Why is he still judge?"

"Well, who else is there to be?" Orwig answered. "He's the only one as knows anythin' about judgin', I guess. 'Sides, there's not a soul in the village as would dare to tell old Jack Williams that he couldn't judge no more."

"Why?" asked Meryl.

"For fear o' his tongue," Irwyn responded. "Old Jack'll tear a strip off yer hide wi' his words, if he hears ye speakin' anythin' that he calls foolishness in his presence. It means folks don't often go to law, so there really isn't much judgin' work to be done. Which suits old Jack just fine, 'cause it leaves him more time for his roses."

"Roses!" exclaimed Meryl, Halstatt, Leaflighter and Heini in unison. The scarecrows blinked in surprise at the unexpected reaction.

"Yes, roses is right," said Orwig doubtfully. "Ye know, them pretty flowers with the nice smell and the thorns and all."

"Of course we know what roses are," Meryl said impatiently. "It's just that they keep turning up on this quest, that's all." She turned to Halstatt. "Could this help us?"

"Hmm," said the draoi.

"Of course it will help!" Heini cried. "We can approach him as fellow rose-lovers, which will make him immediately sympathetic to our cause — or rather, the cause of our esteemed companions."

"And when we tell him of the magic rose, he might want to come with us to Avalon!" Leaflighter shrieked in delight.

"Absolutely not!" chorused the mabinog and the draoi. "We don't have time to travel with an eighty-five-year-old man," Meryl explained to the fairy.

"Stick-in-the-mud," was her predictable response.

"You'd better believe it," Meryl shot back.

"Now, now, let's not get carried away," Heini said soothingly. "No one's going to ask dear old Judge Williams to go to Avalon with us." He threw Leaflighter a quelling look as he said this. "However, we can use the story to soften his attitude towards us, as I said before. I suggest that we approach him in his garden, tell him about your quest, then explain the situation of the scarecrows. He'll be so impressed with us that he'll grant you your jobs back straightaway."

"Just appear in his garden, hmm? A member of the fairy folk, a mabinog, two scarecrows, a motley fool and my own honourable yet admittedly unusual person will suddenly appear in an octogenarian's place of repose. There we shall stun him with the description of a scheme which has grown increasingly ludicrous even to ourselves, and then demand that he restore our colleagues to their former employment, all in the name of justice and because we happen to be fond of the same type of flower. *Hruumph-nha,*" finished the draoi.

Silence followed the tirade. Meryl looked at Irwyn, who then felt called on to offer his opinion. He stirred himself to action.

"Yes, that's all right. Old Jack Williams hates folks wastin' his time, on account of him likely havin' so little left, ye see. I'm sure he'd find that right entertainin' though, which means he might not bark so loudly."

Halstatt rolled his eyes to the heavens, as though he was either abandoning all hope or offering a silent prayer.

"There, that's settled then," Leaflighter said cheerfully. "Let's get going."

"If he dies of fright, you realize, things might go very badly for us indeed, indeed," the draoi intoned.

No one listened to him; at least, they pretended not to. Very likely the fairy never even heard him.

❧

Old Jack Williams knelt on a rug under the shade of a wide-brimmed straw hat in the garden attached to the back of his fine, rambling and now run-down ancestral home. He was weeding with a small trowel at the base of a luxuriant rosebush laden with heavy pink blooms. He didn't hum a tune, or whistle, or even think a great deal. He was enjoying the smell and texture of the earth, and he wouldn't have dreamed of interrupting the industrious buzz of the bees around him with any noise of his own.

Meryl walked up to him silently. The others remained in the background, waiting for her to first make his acquaintance. It had been decided in each of their minds that Halstatt's warning made sense, so when Meryl volunteered to go first, as the least eccentric member of the troupe, everyone readily agreed. Leaflighter made some fuss, wanting a more dramatic opening to their first brush with the law, but practicality won in the end.

"I don't want any tea just yet, Agnes," said Judge Williams without turning round. "I've told you any number of times that I'll call you when I want it."

"Ah," said Meryl, who was suddenly and irrationally afraid she'd be accused of impersonating poor Agnes.

At that, Judge Williams did turn around. Dark brown eyes glared up at her from an impossibly wrinkled face. "You're not Agnes," he said.

"No, no, I didn't say I was, or even think it, sir. I don't even know who Agnes is. I didn't mean to pretend I was her, I promise you." She bit her lip when she realized how odd she must sound.

The brown eyes stared her into silence. "Well, since we're both agreed that you are not Agnes, may I be so bold as to inquire who you are?"

"I'm Meryl, sir. I'm a questing mabinog."

There was a broad pause.

"I'm on my way to Avalon to find a magic rose."

The pause thickened.

"I'm in a bit of a hurry, on account of a possible fairy curse hanging over my head, so I won't waste much of your time."

"How very good of you."

"Yes, so I'll just introduce you to my friends and explain the problem, and then we'll be on our way."

"I see."

"They're a bit unusual, but quite safe."

"That's most comforting to know."

Meryl, at this point mired in desperate humiliation, turned and bellowed, "You can come out, now!" in the direction of the garden gate.

Leaflighter leaped over the hedge and gave the astonished judge a low bow. "Leaflighter of the Twlwyth Teg at your service," she said in her most polite tones. Heini ushered in the cowering scarecrows, who bowed respectfully. The draoi was the last to appear, looking as stony as it was possible for a near-plant to look.

"Please, allow me to make proper introductions," Meryl said, trying her best to recover her poise. "This is Leaflighter, of the fairy folk as she said, but she's harmless enough —"

"I resent that," Leaflighter interjected.

"— this is Heini Heilin, court fool to King Coel. This is Halstatt, a draoi and companion on my quest. And these are Irwyn and Orwig, former members of your village, on whose behalf we come to you now."

The Honourable Judge Williams rose from his knees, shook out the rug on which he had been kneeling, folded it neatly over one arm, then said, "I think we had all better go inside. I believe I would like my tea now, after all."

He removed his straw hat and led them into a darkened study, still warm from the recently departed beam of sunshine that now reached only to the sill of the open window. "Tea for seven, Agnes," he called down a hallway before shutting the door behind him. He looked piercingly at the group huddled in the centre of the room. "Sit down," he said brusquely. He went to a wardrobe and took out an ancient black robe, which he deftly shook out and put on before seating himself behind a heavy table covered with neat stacks of books and papers.

Everyone sat gingerly on the various chairs about the room, with the exception of Leaflighter, who threw herself down upon a small couch in a corner. There she pulled down one of the judge's law books and began leafing through its solemn pages, snickering occasionally. Halstatt tried to glare her into silence, but the fairy simply stuck her tongue out at him. Orwig and Irwyn nervously sat themselves on two stiff-backed chairs placed directly in front of the judge's table. It was obvious that they were terrified of Judge Williams.

"So, you boys are back again, after leaving your family in a fine state of distress," Judge Williams began.

"Aye, yer honour, it be a time of great distress indeed," Irwyn replied.

"We're become desperate men," Orwig added hopefully.

"So I see," the old judge answered, casting a significant glance at Heini's attire. Leaflighter cackled approvingly.

"We been wronged, yer honour, and we're come to set it straight," Irwyn said.

"It seems to me," the judge said, glaring directly at the brothers, "that you might have avoided a lot of bother and trouble by doing so right away. I've little patience for people who don't face up to the consequences of their actions." He glared even more fiercely, drawing his brows together in a grim, grey line across his forehead. Meryl thought he looked exactly like a cross old eagle. She was glad she wasn't on the receiving end of his judgement.

The brothers were hanging their heads shamefacedly. "It's that sorry we are," Irwyn began. "We neither of us were wantin' to cause trouble. We left so's that our family might be spared."

"Spared! Spared what? The truth? Spare the truth and spoil the life, that's what I say — not that anyone bothers to listen, or think about what it means. I don't suppose that you stopped to think it might be worse for your poor mother to have you considered cowards as well as lazy louts, hmm?"

Meryl's gaze went from the judge to the draoi. Halstatt was staring at Jack Williams with open admiration and amazement, while the judge was tapping the tabletop with his fingers in irritation. Again she looked at the draoi and suddenly found herself smothering a laugh. The two, for all their differences, could have been brothers!

"Well?" the judge barked. "Don't just sit there like lumps. If you've anything to say in your own defence, say it now. And mind that you tell the whole truth. I don't have the time to winkle it out of you, you understand?"

The door to the study opened, revealing a small, dark-haired, black-eyed woman carrying a tray of steaming mugs. "She could teach the bards at the Hall a thing or two about restraining emotion," Meryl thought as she watched the woman. "She didn't even blink when she saw Halstatt." The judge took his, then the others followed suit, though neither of the scarecrows took more than a sip of theirs.

The brothers stammered out their story and their suspicions. Every time Heini tried to interject, in a spirit of helpfulness, the judge would bellow, "Quiet, sirrah! Save your breath to cool your porridge. Each man tells his own tale in my court."

"Hmph," the judge said, when the brothers got to the end of their story. He sat back and eyed them expressionlessly. "What I want to know," he said finally, "is what you did with yourselves between the time you fled your home and now, when you appear in my chambers with this accusation against young Davey Owens and a whole horde of strangers backing you up."

The brothers looked at one another helplessly. Heini opened his mouth to speak but shut it again at one look from the judge. Leaflighter began to guffaw loudly, while Halstatt took on a noble and long-suffering expression. Meryl poked the fairy and hissed "Be quiet!" at her. Leaflighter poked her back, mouthing "Stick-in-the-mud."

Leaflighter chose that moment to pour her tea down a mousehole. Meryl hoped, desperately, that the judge hadn't noticed. She lifted her feet off the floor as the mouse came streaking across it, heading straight for Orwig's chair. The fairy watched it hiding between his feet with wicked interest. Silently, Meryl resolved to murder her later on.

"Well?" prompted the judge.

"As I said afore, we was desperate men," Orwig began hopefully.

"Ah yes, the cry of the cowardly and irresponsible," the judge growled.

Irwyn flushed scarlet. "We weren't no cowards," he said hotly. "We was driven to try a life of crime, it's true, but we never hurt no one."

"A life of crime that *never hurt no one* has never existed and will never exist," the judge said slowly, grinding his words like glass between his teeth. "Just what form did this life of crime take?"

The brothers shuffled their feet against the carpet, each of them speechless, until Orwig yelped, leaped to his feet and began to shriek. Leaflighter hooted with delight, and the others began gabbling with confusion, while Meryl ushered the offending mouse back to his hole with her foot, jabbing the fairy a second time with her finger.

The judge pounded his desk and yelled, "Order, order! Behave yourselves, the pack of you!"

"It was only a mouse," Meryl said to the trembling scarecrow.

"You," said the judge, pointing at Orwig. "Let's have no more of these outbursts. I don't care if a plague of mice is running over your toes. Now tell me, while I still have breath in my body and some measure of patience left, just exactly what crime did you sorry pair undertake?" He glowered and folded his arms across his chest as he waited.

"Well, sir, we come upon this oracle here, sleepin' in the forest, and we minded how our granny said as how an oracle could tell you things as what was goin' to happen —"

"A common misconception, which I studiously tried to point out to them, *hruumph-nha*," Halstatt interjected primly.

The judge waved his hand impatiently for the scarecrow to continue.

"Well, sir, we thought as how an oracle could tell us of any rich folks travellin' on the road — mean rich folk, like as who never share their goods with anyone," Orwig added hastily, seeing the scowl deepen on the judge's face.

"And you thought to share their wealth with them whether they liked it or not, is that what you're telling me?" Judge Williams demanded.

"Only the mean ones," Irwyn added again.

"Mean by whose judgement? And why do you think a mean man should suffer while a generous man should not? And what did you think to do if only kind men came along? And how do you point your finger at the follies of young Davey and expect me to wink at your own, hmm?" The judge took another sip of his tea, sat back in his chair, and looked at the brothers as though they were aphids on his finest rosebush. The scarecrows squirmed in their seats.

A suspicion crept into Meryl's mind. "Sir," she said, somewhat nervously, "you said 'the follies of young Davey' just now. Do you mean ... I mean to say, is it ..."

"Well?" said the judge, impatient with her stammering.

"Sir, does everyone know what really happened?" Meryl asked bluntly.

"Of course they do. Not everyone runs away from their trouble. Take young Davey, for example. It seems he felt that you had been lording your position over his father, so he thought to take your pride down a notch or two. He managed to convince your sister Mary to let him carry you your noon meal, and he put something in your beer to make you sleepy. He's no doctor, so he used far too much of the drug, with the result that you slept much longer than he had intended. Fortunately, I suppose, he didn't use so much that you never woke again. He gave himself a proper scare when he saw how much damage he'd done, and how thoughtless he'd been. It scared him into being a better man, I hope. The truth didn't come out of him until after you had left. Mary came to him in a fine state of feminine distress, and he confessed to her, then together they came to me. As for your jobs, you'll have to go to Sir Rodric. He was sorry that he'd acted so hastily, once the truth came out."

"So Mary guessed his guilt, did she? She always were a bright girl, our Mary," Irwyn stated proudly.

"Hmm, yes, well, bright she may be, but she went to see young Davey because of their mutual affection," Judge Williams replied.

The brothers' mouths fell open. "Affection!" bellowed Orwig. "Affection for the very devil what robbed us of our work an' our good names!"

"Well, he certainly didn't rob you of your voices," the judge remarked tersely. "As for your good names, you'd do well to take better care of those than you have done recently."

Meryl couldn't help feeling sorry for the scarecrows. "Judge Williams," she asked, "if you knew Irwyn and Orwig were framed, why did you make them explain themselves?"

The judge turned his piercing glare upon her, making Meryl instantly regret her question. She stood her ground, however, and forced herself to look back into the old eagle's eyes.

"So you think I'm harsh, do you?" he barked at her.

"Well, a bit," she replied tentatively.

"A bit!" he snorted. "A bit! Don't wimble your words, youngster, or you'll never be a bard. Isn't that what a mabinog wants to be?"

Meryl nodded dumbly.

"What, now you can't speak at all?" the judge scoffed.

"Yes, I can speak. Yes, I want to be a bard. And yes, I think you're an old ogre," Meryl snapped back, her temper rising.

"That's more like it," the judge said approvingly. "I make every man, woman and child who comes before me plead their case. Say what you think, after you've thought about what you should say. Once people start thinking, they usually come to the conclusion that there's nothing like the truth to get them out of a sticky situation. And truth, my dear girl," he said, looking at her with a level gaze, "truth is what I seek, always."

The door to the study opened again, and Agnes reappeared.

"Ah, Agnes, well timed. Kindly collect the tea things and then see to the meal, will you? I think we shall be having guests at supper." The small woman nodded, and picked up the mugs.

When Agnes had departed, the judge turned his attention back to the brothers. "I think it best that you make your way home. Your mother has been in a sad state since your departure, and young Mary hasn't known which way to turn. Young Davey and his father pulled together to replant the lost fields, and there's still summer enough that all may not be lost."

The scarecrows shambled to their feet.

The judge continued, "If I may give you some advice, good men, I suggest that you quickly forgive young Davey his foolish act. It's Mary who will suffer if you don't. If it sticks in your craw, just remember that neither of you is a paragon of virtue. I hope you'll be better men for knowing it, too. Good day," he finished abruptly.

The brothers left, after wringing each of their companions' hands in gratitude. Leaflighter tweaked both their noses, but they didn't seem to mind too much. They accidentally snapped off two of Halstatt's fingers in the process, but they apologized so profusely that he hardly grumbled at all. Finally they left, bowing as they backed out the door. A heavy silence descended. The judge leaned back in his chair and gazed at the others.

"So," he said finally, "tell me about this magical rose."

Meryl was startled by the twinkle she saw in the dark depths of his eyes.

CHAPTER SEVENTEEN

THE DRAOI, THE FAIRY AND THE FOOL all turned to Meryl. She glared at them in return, took a deep breath and jumped into the story of their adventure — though by the time each member of the party had had his or her say it was hard to know who was telling the story and who was interrupting. By the end of the tale Meryl had a headache, Heini was growing hoarse, and Halstatt had pulled out several leaves in frustration. Only Leaf-lighter was still grinning, sitting cross-legged on her couch like an evil red gnome. She loved it when things got loud.

The door to the study opened. "The meal is ready, sir," said Agnes.

"Excellent," replied the judge. "Please follow me."

He lead them through the narrow passage to a small dining chamber furnished with a large table surrounded by eight heavy chairs. There was a fireplace at one end of the room, but it had no fire. As if to compensate, the late-afternoon sun shone in from windows on two adjoining walls. The wood of the furniture was dark, the light a deep gold; it was a very sombre room.

They sat down to a full meal of cold roast meats, fresh bread, cheese and wine. "You must pardon my ignorance," the judge said to his guests. "Neither Agnes nor I am familiar with the culinary tastes of the Twlwyth Teg or a draoi. Is there anything in particular you require?" He looked graciously from one to another.

"Milk," Leaflighter said promptly. "And perhaps some oat porridge would be nice," she added cheerfully. "In honour of our dear departed scarecrow friends, you see." She smiled brightly at the judge.

"Perhaps some camomile tea?" Halstatt asked hopefully. "Really, what I need most is a good drink. If you could throw in some dirt it would make it really capital."

Judge Williams nodded to Agnes.

"Milk, oat porridge and camomile-dirt tea," she said, still without expression. "Right away, sir."

"It's a most surprising tale you've brought me today — of roses and oracles, a quest and the Twlwyth Teg," the judge said pleasantly, offering Meryl a large helping of roast goose. "I haven't been so agreeably annoyed in quite some time, I must say."

"We didn't mean to annoy you," Meryl hastened to add.

The judge waved her comment away dismissively. "Everything except gardening annoys me, these days. There was a time when the endless bickerings among my fellow mortals held a certain fascination for me. There was even a time — long ago now, longer almost than memory — when I felt a passion to right the wrongs of the world. But now I'm tired of sorting out troubles for people too lazy to do it themselves. I ask only to be left in peace among my roses."

"At least you've kept your teeth," Leaflighter announced brightly.

"Leaflighter!" Meryl groaned, "What on earth —?"

"Most mortals don't," the fairy said, puzzled by the reaction her words had sparked. "I'd be surprised if either of you do, even supposing you live as long as our host here. Old Barky over there doesn't need to worry, though." She grinned affably at the draoi.

"Physical health is a great gift," the judge replied dryly.

At that moment Agnes reappeared, and the fairy's attention turned to her stomach. Meryl sent Heini a look of relief. She was irritated to discover him grinning into his wine pot.

"So tell me," the judge said evenly as he passed Meryl the bread, "how do you intend to prove to the Queen that your quest justifies your breaking of the fairy law?"

Meryl took a piece of bread and passed the plate on to Heini. "I haven't thought much about it." She looked up from her plate to find the judge's eagle eyes upon her. Meryl heard the echo of her own words and blushed to the roots of her hair.

"I mean, of course I've thought about it," she said quickly. "I thought, that is, Halstatt and I thought —"

The draoi sniffed contemptuously.

"Well, I thought that when we arrived at the shores of Avalon we'd just sort of ask the Queen to let us come to her to explain how we accidentally brought iron on the Way." Meryl knew it was a poor excuse for a plan, and she threw Halstatt an irritated look.

"Yes, I think I do see," the judge said shortly. "I see that you're leaving the result of one of the most important trials of your life to chance and another's good opinion of your intentions. Is that so?"

Meryl was taken aback. "We argued our case to the King. He's the one who left the decision to the Queen. It's out of our hands, now."

"Out of your hands!" The judge thumped the table with his knife, making all the dishes rattle and his guests jump in their seats. "What a sorry attitude that is. Do you think you are in the right, or not?"

"I hope so," Meryl stammered.

"Not good enough!" thundered the judge. "Why let others decide your fate? Face the truth head on, girl. If you were wrong to break the fairy law, then submit to the King's punishment. If you were guilty of gross impertinence, then take your medicine and learn from it. If you were right, then *prove it* to the Queen, do you hear me? Don't go wringing your hands at her gate hoping she'll prove it to you. What sort of namby-pamby bard would you be, waiting for others to pat you on the head and tell you that you've got a story worth hearing, hmm? You convince them, that's what you do!"

"A good point," Heini said. Meryl turned on him with a glare. "Well, it *is* a good point," he said innocently, as he stuffed his mouth with goose.

"And how do you think to discover the truth about Taliesin's supposed crime if you can't decide about your own, hmm?" the judge demanded.

"I know the truth about myself!" Meryl declared hotly.

"Then what is it? Let's hear what you know." The judge sat back in his chair and stared at her over a cold roast of venison.

Meryl flushed angrily. "You can't bully me the way you bullied the scarecrows. I know what you're trying to do. You're trying to get me to think clearly," she snapped.

Leaflighter gave a loud laugh. "And she doesn't appreciate it, your honour!" she crowed delightedly.

Meryl's blush deepened, and she felt tears of frustration spring to her eyes. She flung her gaze up defiantly at the judge and was once again thrown off balance by the twinkle in his eyes.

Sheepishly she grinned. "That's not what I mean," she began again.

"Then say what you mean."

"What I mean is, I know that Taliesin must have had a good reason for taking the rose," she said.

"Why?" asked the judge.

"Because he was the greatest bard in history!"

"So? Since when does being a great storyteller prevent one from being a greedy thief?" Judge Williams asked coldly.

Meryl floundered for a moment, then recovered. "I know about Taliesin!" she declared passionately. "I've read his book. He wanted to inspire people to be the best they could be. He worked for King Arthur, and he encouraged people to search for the grail. He believed his life should be spent in service, promoting the good in people and the health of the land. He couldn't have been a greedy thief!" She paused for breath, her heart pounding in her ears.

The judge merely regarded her impassively. "And what if he was?" he asked her. "Would that make his achievements less great, or his ideals less worthy?"

"No," Meryl said slowly, "but they'd be tainted, somehow, if he was less honourable than I thought."

"Really?" Judge Williams leaned forward to examine her face closely. "Think for a moment about your favourite stories. Are the heroes perfect? Are the heroines spotless?"

Meryl thought for a moment. "Well, no. The perfect ones are always a bit dull and colourless. But I don't see what that has to do with Taliesin," she added firmly.

"Of course you do, or you would if you'd think. The best tales are full of conflict, with characters who make mistakes and learn from them. Now what about Taliesin? Did he steal the rose? Why did he do it? Was he sorry for his crime? Did he learn from it, or was it his great failing? It made you think, didn't it? It made you spring into action. It gave you a direction and a goal you could grab. It gave you Avalon. In short, it forced you to take risks, risks that will break you or make you stronger. Well?"

Meryl was dazed. "I guess so ..." she began.

"Don't guess, think! Tell the Queen that you've come to learn the truth about Taliesin, and mean it. If it should prove that he was a greedy fellow when it came to roses — a failing I can well sympathize with, I might add — then that should give you hope."

"In what way?" Meryl asked limply. She felt as though she had spent the supper hour being mauled by a bear.

"If he's less than perfect, he's more like you. So if he can be great, why then, so can you! Do you see?" He sat back in his chair, evidently well pleased with himself.

"But he became great after drinking from the cauldron of Ceridwen," Meryl objected. "If I don't get to Avalon I won't have that opportunity."

"Work, study, think," trumpeted the judge. "That's what will make you a bard, not any magic cauldron, mark my words. You march to Avalon and state your case clearly. Tell the truth and face the truth. If he's a thief, he's a thief. If he's not, he's not. If you're meant to be a bard, be a bard. If not, then be something else. But whatever you do, don't fuss and fret and wimble. Then, no matter what judgement you receive, you'll know it's what you've earned, not what you've been granted."

Meryl sat very still. Her ears burned. Leaflighter grinned at her from across the table, a white ring of milk drying around her lips. Heini stared at the ceiling and began to hum an aimless tune.

"Oh," said Meryl.

Agnes came into the room, took one stern look at the judge and said, "You look weary, sir. You're not to tire yourself, remember."

"Yes, yes," he said pettishly. "You are all welcome to stay the night," he told his guests. "Agnes will manage, and I would like to hear more about that magical rose of yours."

"We'll bring it back to show you," Meryl offered somewhat rashly. "Or at any rate, we'll bring you news of it. But as for staying, I think we'll say no." She looked at each of her companions. None protested; they were all watching her. "We've still got some evening light, and it would be best to leave the village before the news gets out that you've got a fairy and a draoi staying with you. Irwyn and Orwig are good men, but they do tend to boast of their adventures."

Old Judge Williams nodded. "I will look for your return," he said gravely. "Allow me to show you out."

He led them back to the garden. The heady scent of roses filled the evening air. Agnes reappeared one last time as they were shaking hands, carrying a large paper package. "Food for your trip," she said curtly to Meryl. "I didn't think you'd object, sir."

"Of course not, Agnes. Thank you, that's quite right."

Everyone said their thanks, except for Leaflighter, who threw her arms around the judge's neck and gave his cheek a hearty kiss. Meryl was horrified, but the judge only said, "Bless my soul!" and looked oddly pleased. The mabinog decided that by now she shouldn't be surprised by anything the fairy did.

Halstatt shook the judge's hand and paid him the highest compliment he could bestow. "You're a credit to your species," he said fervently. "A more draoi-like mortal I've never met."

The judge bowed solemnly in reply, but Meryl saw that twinkle in his eye again. "He's a contradictory character himself," she thought.

Meryl was the last to leave, as she had been the first to arrive. She shuffled her feet a bit, at a loss for words.

Old Jack Williams looked at her quietly. He glanced around his garden. "Will you allow an old judge to give you one more piece of advice before you go?"

Meryl nodded.

"When you're faced with that magical cauldron, do what you believe is right and true. Listen to your conscience as well as your heart."

"I will," Meryl vowed.

"And remember, when it comes to be your turn to judge, let justice guide your own ruling."

"When will I be a judge?" Meryl asked, puzzled.

"When the facts of Taliesin's theft lie before you, of course."

Meryl stared at him. "I hadn't thought of myself as his judge," she said slowly. "I just want to know the truth."

He smiled at her, brilliantly, and he suddenly looked young. "You have learned, then. There is hope for us all."

They shook hands. Meryl went off into the twilight, and old Judge Williams turned back into his house.

CHAPTER EIGHTEEN

T HEY ARRIVED AT A WAY-POINT sometime before noon the next day. There they stopped to eat another meal and fill their flasks at a spring before jumping onto the fairy Way and setting out for Avalon, at last. Leaflighter tried to convince Meryl to leave behind her rose clasp, but the mabinog wouldn't hear of it.

"I've been on the Way with iron before, and I'll go on it with iron again," she insisted.

"Yes, but then you didn't know it was a fairy crime," Leaflighter argued.

"Well, if it weren't for your 'high jinks', as Halstatt calls it, we would have been at Avalon by now and the case would be decided. If I have to bring it on a second time that's your fault, not mine."

"Stick-in-the-mud," Leaflighter grumbled. But she brought the entire group, iron clasp and all, onto the Way nonetheless.

The Way was as sunny and cheerful as ever. Heini kept sniffing the air, claiming that he could smell the magic all around them. Meryl couldn't smell anything. The others said that was because she was purely mortal, and she tried not to feel left out. Both Halstatt and Meryl walked with an air of studied nonchalance, each trying to ignore the fact that every step brought them closer to their potential doom. Leaflighter skipped along merrily, which was just what everyone expected of her.

It was obvious that something had gone terribly wrong, therefore, when the fairy abruptly broke off her singing and stared around her with a look of worried concentration.

"What is it?" Meryl asked. Her nerves began to fail her. "Is it the King? Is he angry because we left the Way? Remember, that was all your idea —"

"Be quiet!" Leaflighter hissed. "I can't listen properly with all your nattering."

The group waited tensely as Leaflighter listened to the silence of the Way.

"Can you hear anything?" Meryl whispered to Halstatt at one point. He shook his head. Leaflighter growled at her to be quiet again.

Finally the fairy spoke. "There's something wrong on our dancing green," she explained, "though I can't tell exactly what. All I can hear is a jumble of angry voices."

"Well, perhaps the court is just disagreeing over which dance to do next," Heini suggested helpfully.

"Fairies don't argue," Leaflighter said, anxiously. Halstatt snorted at that. "I mean, with one another," she added.

"What should we do?" Meryl hoped that she wouldn't come to regret the question.

"We'd better take a look," the fairy decided.

"Hazelnuts and horsefeathers, the last thing we need to do right now is get involved in some sort of fairy brawl," Halstatt muttered.

In her heart Meryl agreed with the draoi. "But Leaflighter says that the fairies shouldn't be fighting," she pointed out faintly, nonetheless.

"No doubt, no doubt indeed. However, we are already on the shady side of His Majesty's graces, and I don't think interrupting a domestic quarrel will improve our standing with the fairy court, if you see what I mean, *hruumph-nhá*."

It was Heini who leaped to Leaflighter's defence. "We're all in this together!" he cried valiantly, without any clear understanding of what "this" was.

They likely would have stood there arguing for days if Leaflighter hadn't lost patience and swept them all off the Way. The last thing Meryl noticed before the Way vanished was Halstatt screeching, "May I remind you that you are not the individual facing an eternity of root rot!" into Heini's implacable face.

The dancing green, a bright glade in the midst of the gloomy forest where the fairy court held its summer revels, was a mass of confusion. Red, blue, white and green fairies were everywhere, intermingled with what appeared to be a host of tiny rabbits. Gwyn ap Nudd was actually standing on his throne, his crown askew. It looked as though he was shouting at one rabbit in particular. Meryl shook her head to clear it when it seemed as though the rabbit was shouting back.

"May I borrow this?" Heini bellowed into Meryl's face. He had his hand on her staff. Meryl nodded dazedly and gave it to him.

The fool strode into the centre of the roaring chaos. There he stuck Meryl's staff firmly into the ground and proceeded to swing around it, like a crazed Morris dancer. That caught the attention of enough of the surrounding fairies and rabbits that his cries of "Hear ye, hear ye!" could eventually be heard over the general hubbub. It was not long before he held everyone's fixed attention.

"Your most gracious Majesty," said Heini, making a low, sweeping bow to the astonished King of the Twlwyth Teg. "My companions and I were journeying along your magical Way on our voyage to Avalon when we noted a disturbance in your midst. Immediately we abandoned our course to offer you any assistance we might be capable of, and we now stand here ready, awaiting your command." He swept the King another bow, his eyes twinkling. It was obvious that he was enormously proud of his impromptu speech.

At that moment Meryl made a startling realization. The "rabbits" were actually very tiny people, the tallest less than one foot in height, dressed entirely in brown furry skins.

"Who are they?" she whispered to Halstatt.

"I have no idea," he muttered back.

Meryl stared at him in amazement; she'd thought the draoi knew everything.

"Who," intoned the King in a thunderous voice, "are you?"

Heini paled slightly but continued bravely. "I am Heini Heilin, court fool to the honourable and heavy-handed Coel, on a pilgrimage to a kinder, sweeter kingdom. On that anthill to our rear are my worthy companions, with whom I believe you are already acquainted." He bowed once more, this time with more fear and less flourish.

Meryl leaped off the anthill in question, as did Leaflighter and Halstatt. The King turned his stony glare upon them. "Has the trial been completed?" he bellowed. He had only just noticed that his crown was crooked, and it made his mood even more foul, if that was possible.

"Ah, well ..." began Leaflighter. Fortunately she was interrupted by the rabbit-person who stood before the throne.

"What is the meaning of all this?" it squeaked in an angry voice. "Is this some ploy to divert our attention or muddle the issue at hand? Because it won't work, I tell you; the Faylinn are not so easily fooled."

The King turned his angry countenance back to the rabbit-person, and the shouting recommenced.

"The Faylinn!" exclaimed Halstatt.

"You know them now?" Meryl asked. She was almost relieved to hear it.

"Of course, though I never would have expected to find them here. Their kingdom is in the west of Eire. My mother told me of them. My grandfather was highly regarded by their people, indeed, indeed he was."

"Do you think you can do anything to sort this out, then? Because if you can, it might save our skins. It doesn't look as though Leaflighter is going to be much help."

The fairy had joined some other red Twlwyth Teg and thrown herself into the argument with high good humour. She was the only fairy present who clearly felt the whole ruckus was a marvellous lark.

The draoi began to carefully wend his way to the throne. Heini had begun his bizarre staff dance again, but it didn't seem to be having any effect this time. Meryl wished, desperately, that she could simply disappear.

Halstatt arrived at the side of the rabbit-person embroiled in argument with the King. Meryl watched him shrieking an introduction; at least that's what she supposed he was doing. Certainly whatever he said caught their attention. Even Gwyn ap Nudd stopped shouting and listened. There were a few moments of conversation, during which Halstatt did most of the talking. Then the King nodded, as did the rabbit-person. Meryl couldn't decide whether the draoi looked relieved or terrified.

The King sat down upon his throne. There was a horrendous clap of thunder, and a blade of lightning cut across the sky. The shouting ceased abruptly and all eyes turned towards him.

"This fern-friend," said Gwyn ap Nudd, gesturing towards Halstatt, "has offered to intercede as mediator in our debate. I and King ... Iubdan" — here it looked as though he was chewing on something hideously sour — "have agreed to this. We shall proceed at once."

"Ah, yes," Halstatt began, clearly terrified. "First, we shall hear from the complainant."

Both Gwyn ap Nudd and the rabbit-person began to speak.

For a tense moment it looked as though everyone would begin shouting again, but Halstatt took control.

"Ah, right then. First we need to establish *who* the complainant *is*. Starting with your Majesty," here he nodded to Gwyn ap Nudd, "would you each state the problem, briefly, as you see it."

Meryl sat down, along with the rest of the crowd. She had begun to be interested, in spite of her fear. Heini moved beside her.

The King nodded sternly. "My people and I arrived upon this green but a short while ago, to commence our usual feasting. To our surprise, we found it covered in small tents, with the construction of a fortification under way in the very place where my throne usually resides. Naturally we took immediate action. We wiped the traces of such rubbish from our hallowed place and gave a stern warning to the perpetrators to flee lest they be cursed unto nine generations. Yet they stayed, and would quarrel, and ... I *demand* they go away," he finished bluntly.

The fairies cheered. Halstatt waited for silence, then turned to King Iubdan. "You may now present your case."

King Iubdan was clearly a dramatic fellow, his small stature notwithstanding. He assumed a pompous stance and turned a tragic countenance upon his listeners. "See, see my wandering, homeless people!" he cried, making a theatrical gesture with his arms. A sigh rose up from the crowd.

Meryl and Heini leaned forward to catch every nuance of the performance. They both were convinced that they were watching a Master at work.

"Long ago, when still we dwelled in our fair land, I made a boast that none were as mighty a people as the Faylinn. For this my poet — Eisirt was the traitor's name — sought to have me humbled, for in my pride I had declared myself, who ruled over such a grand race, the mightiest ruler that ever lived. The traitor Eisirt travelled to the land of the north, where lived a race of giants. One of these he brought back to my court and paraded there for all to see. 'Look at how our mighty king fades in his shadow!' Eisirt cried, and true it was that in stature I was far beneath this Aedh of the north. But 'Might is no mere measure of height, nor is greatness a matter of inches!' I cried. 'My people are still the grandest in the land, and I their stalwart king!'"

King Iubdan paused to wipe his brow with a ridiculously small handkerchief. Then he continued, his voice full of passion.

"The false Eisirt then laughed and challenged me to travel back to the northern land with this Aedh. He put a geis on me that I be the first to taste the porridge set down before their king, Fergus Mac Leide." The crowd gasped.

"What's a geis?" Meryl hissed to Heini. He shrugged. "Remind me to ask Halstatt," she grumbled.

"I travelled far, in the company of the giant Aedh and my lovely wife, Queen Bebo. The honour of my people hung heavy on my shoulders, and the weight of the geis pulled at my heart. But still we travelled on, until we came to the land where the very ground trembled at every step the giants made. Aedh, who was small among his people, took pity upon us and brought us within the palace undetected. In the morning, I, with my beloved Bebo at my side, went to the breakfast hall and drew myself upon the monstrous table. Victory was within my grasp! With the help of Bebo I lifted myself to the rim of the bowl and reached for the porridge. It was then that tragedy struck. A sentinel, alerted to our presence, set up such a cry that the entire hall rumbled with the sound of the giants' voices. In the tumult I slipped into the porridge, drawing my unfortunate, wailing Bebo behind me."

The crowd moaned. One lone snicker was heard, which was quickly hushed, though not before Meryl recognized the voice as Leaflighter's.

"For a year and a day we were kept as hostages of King Fergus, my faithful wife constantly subjected to his horrendous advances. Finally we were told that we could buy our freedom. The price would be the ancient treasure of the Faylinn, the magical shoes that allow the wearer to walk across water as easily as though it were dry land. In sorrow we agreed, for I knew that my people needed me, their ruler, more than any treasure. The agreement was made, and home I returned with my Bebo, she lamenting all the way. When we arrived back in our fair land there was great rejoicing, save in the heart of the false Eisirt. Yet my heart was heavy-laden, for I knew the price at which I'd won back my kingdom."

Here King Iubdan raised his arms to the crowd in appeal. "When I told you, my people, there were many among you who were fell with wrath at the cost, and yet all but Eisirt came to my side in the end. Then the false Faylinn saw that he had lost all, for truly he had held it in his heart that he should become king in my place. In jealousy he slipped away at night, travelling back to the land of the north, to the land of the giants. Then saw we all how we had been betrayed, and we swore that when the northern dogs came for the shoes that we would deny them, for we felt that they had been unfairly won through the trickery of the false Eisirt."

The crowd grumbled in agreement.

"When the court of giants came for the shoes we told them nay, and said, 'Look to your traitor Faylinn friend for the reason!' and refused to say anymore, though they pleaded with us for days. Back to the north they went, empty-handed, and great rejoicing was known again in our land. But those good days were few, for soon the giants came, a war host full wroth. Our lands were taken, our homes destroyed, and we were cast out to wander with nothing but our very lives and the magic shoes. For those they did not take, nor will they ever, though they chase us to the ends of the earth!"

A cheer went up; Meryl was astounded to find her own voice joining in. It took Halstatt a while to reclaim everyone's attention.

"Yes, a woeful story, indeed, indeed," Halstatt intoned to King Iubdan. "However, it doesn't really address the problem at hand. You've apparently set up shop, to use a rather ridiculous human expression, on the dancing green of the Tylwyth Teg, if you see what I mean, *hruumph-nha.*"

The King of the Faylinn looked rather nonplussed. "We can wander no farther. Our spirits flag within us. This is ideal as a land for our new home, and ... and ... there was no one here when we arrived." Determined, he jutted his jaw, and the Faylinn muttered in agreement. Gwyn ap Nudd looked as though he were going to have an apoplectic fit and began to splutter. Halstatt hastily stepped in again.

"Now then, we see that you need a home, and we're all reasonable creatures here — or at any rate I am a reasonable creature and that will suffice for the moment, *hruumph-nha.* Here is the difficulty, you see. You simply assumed that because there was no one on the green at the time you discovered it, that it was unowned, or at any rate unused. Correct?"

King Iubdan nodded in surly agreement.

"Well then, your mistake must have become evident when the fairy court arrived upon the green, if you see what I mean, *hruumph-nha.*"

"We thought they were agents of the northern hounds, come once again to shatter our peace!" the Faylinn monarch cried.

"Yes, well, I can certainly see how that mistake could be made, indeed, indeed I do, having been in the company of a horde of howling fairies on several occasions now, with all due respect to

Your Majesty," he added quickly, looking to Gwyn ap Nudd. "Nonetheless, the mistake has been clarified, and now we must resolve the matter at hand."

There was a weighty silence, which was finally broken by the King of the Tylwyth Teg. "Resolve it then, tree-twin. We're waiting upon you."

Halstatt gasped and choked a bit, and then found his voice. "Well now, clearly the Faylinn should not have begun construction without first ascertaining whether or not the land they were building upon was owned." The fairies began to cheer and the Faylinn to wail. Halstatt raised his arms and shouted for silence. He was getting quite good at controlling a crowd, Meryl noted.

"Of course," and here Halstatt glared at the riotous Leaflighter until she silenced herself, "the Tylwyth Teg would have been well advised to speak with the Faylinn before destroying their work. Perhaps, with understanding, a better solution could have been found." Here the Faylinn began to look more cheerful, and the Tylwyth Teg started to mutter.

"In short, I suggest a compromise. Perhaps the Tylwyth Teg would be willing to sell you this land, in exchange for those magical shoes of yours, if you see what I mean." He looked hopefully into the faces of both rulers.

The Faylinn drew to one side of the green, the fairies to the other. A murmur rose from each camp. Halstatt was left alone in the middle, wringing his hands nervously until the twigs rattled, and making every effort to appear calm. Meryl went to his side, for moral support.

"What's a geis?" she asked the draoi.

"Eh?"

She repeated the question and he looked horrified, which Meryl took as a promising sign. If he was busy exclaiming about her education, maybe he'd forget about the trial at hand.

"Really, I don't know how those Masters of yours can sleep at night, I don't indeed, indeed. A geis is a law of fate set on an individual. Think of it as a magically enforced dare that you refuse at your peril. If you break a geis you are cast out of society. In most cases you die a particularly nasty death and are utterly dishonoured. It's taken very seriously, I assure you, *hruumph-nha*."

By now the two groups had finished their discussions. Gravely the monarchs came face to face before Halstatt. Meryl suddenly wished that she had stayed in the crowd with the fool.

Gwyn ap Nudd spoke first. "We have agreed to sell the land for the price agreed upon, providing that we may have our feast here as planned before we journey on to the next green. That will allow us the winter to discover a new green upon which to hold our dance at this time of the year ever after."

King Iubdan conferred quickly and then returned.

"My people also agree to this, though it pains us to finally lose the treasure we have guarded at such a heavy cost. The magic shoes are dear to our hearts, but they have already lost us one home. If they can buy us a second they have paid their debt in full." He bowed graciously to the King of the Tylwyth Teg.

Halstatt beamed in obvious relief. "There now, that's all settled then. You have your dance, then the Faylinn will give you the shoes and send you on your Way, so to speak, and get down to the business of building themselves a new home. Right, then, we'll be off ourselves, indeed, indeed." The draoi began to move away from the kings, bowing and beaming as he did so.

"Not so fast, fern-face," Gwyn ap Nudd said tersely. "Though I thank you for your aid in this situation, there is still the matter of your own trial before us. How is it that your task is not completed?"

Meryl, every fibre of her being quaking in fear, spoke up. "Forgive us, Your Majesty," she began. His Majesty did not look terribly forgiving, but she pressed on. "We were delayed in our quest when your servant, Leaflighter, was injured. We had to seek the help of a fairy doctor, which brought on a whole series of delays, none of which would be of interest to you, I am sure. But we are here again, and our quest has been resumed." She broke off, suspecting that she had already begun to babble.

The King frowned. "One of my people wounded on our Way? How can that be?"

"Oh, it wasn't on the Way," Leaflighter called out gaily from a band of red fairies. "It happened while we were playing a trick on some humans at a wedding. A horrid old fairy midwife hit me with a dart. She very nearly spoiled all the fun." A hiss of anger went up from the troop of fairies; spoiled fun was the thing they hated most.

"I see," said the King. There was a hush as he drummed his fingers on the arm of his throne and considered the trio of mabinog, fool and draoi before him. Finally he spoke again. "I do not like delays, but you have rendered us a service today so I will remain lenient towards you. However, I do not wish this matter to continue between us unresolved. My servant Leaflighter will conduct you to the shores of Avalon by the swiftest of magical routes. I and my people will join you there in three human-time days. Then we shall see how things stand." He smiled grimly and waved them away with his hand.

Immediately the four of them were back on the Way; even the fairy looked flustered.

"Three days," said Meryl. She felt stunned.

"We'd better get moving," Heini said brightly.

Leaflighter led the way.

CHAPTER NINETEEN

"I CAN SEE WHY you're always chasing after excitement," Meryl said to Leaflighter in a grim tone. It was the second day of their march to Avalon. The Way had grown stiller as they approached their goal, so that the seriousness of their journey seemed to be reflected in the atmosphere itself. They calculated the passage of time by their cycles of hunger and need to sleep. "I almost wish it would rain, or a dog would start barking in the distance — it's so quiet it's irritating."

"Humans," sniffed Halstatt.

"Humans, indeed," Heini agreed fervently. "I know exactly what you mean." The fool had removed his jangling cap, because the tinkling of the bells was grating on everyone's nerves, even his own. Leaflighter had grabbed the hat and worn it for awhile, just to be annoying, but she finally wearied of the sport and tossed it back.

The fairy grinned. "Well, that would be a start, old stick-in-the-mud, but a barking dog is hardly my idea of excitement. Now a dragon might be worth considering —"

"No thank you," Meryl said quickly. "I only said I found it quiet; I didn't complain about it being dull. It'll be all too exciting once we get to Avalon, no doubt."

At once the possibility of life without her voice rose in Meryl's mind. Her stomach knotted up. Her adventurous quest was suddenly shadowed by the grim reality of the trial she was facing. She glanced at Halstatt, and pictured him adrift on a boat, suffering root rot because of her. She began to feel distinctly queasy.

"How much longer till we arrive?" Heini asked.

"We're just about there," Leaflighter answered cheerfully.

Now that she was about to reach her long-awaited destination, Meryl had a horrible feeling that she never should have left the Hall in the first place. What was a year of peeling potatoes compared to the wrath of Gwyn ap Nudd? Why had she been so impatient? What if she lost her voice — or worse, became mad? She felt her stomach slide down to her knees and then heave itself up into her throat.

"I think I'm going to be sick," she said.

"You do look a tad green," Heini replied. "What happened to your spirit of adventure?"

"It crawled back to the Hall," the mabinog snapped. She went to the Wayside and promptly threw up.

"Well," said Halstatt dryly, when she had finished, "your spirit of adventure might be gone, but your flair for the dramatic is still very much with you."

"Shut up, Halstatt," Meryl mumbled. She was thoroughly embarrassed.

"Oh, now, don't feel bad," the draoi replied calmly, helping her back to her feet. "I can tell you hundreds of stories of famous heroes who responded to their first taste of danger in exactly the same manner."

"Really?" Meryl said doubtfully. "Who?"

"Ahem, well, these aren't commonly known facts, you see. We draoi tend to keep them to ourselves, knowing how awkward the heroes in question might find it should the tale get out, if you see what I mean, *hruumph-nha*. Suffice it to say that you're in excellent company, and I'll be as silent in your case as I am in all others. And so will you two be as well," he finished, glaring at the fairy and the fool significantly. They nodded solemnly in agreement; even Leaflighter didn't dare smile.

All at once the fairy stopped and closed her eyes, listening for something apparently only she could hear. When she was satisfied, she smiled and turned to Meryl. "Are you ready?" she asked.

The mabinog gulped and then managed a terse "Yes." But she didn't let go of Halstatt's hand, and he didn't complain, even when she accidentally snapped off a twig.

There was a whirl of fairy magic: their sight was dazzled with swirling colours and their hearing beguiled with eerie music, like fairy piping blown on a sorrowing wind. The next thing they knew, they were standing on the sandy shore of a lake. Everything more than an arm's length away was obscured by a heavy mist. The quiet was deeper than it had been on the Way; it sank into their bones.

The lake was so still it made Meryl's skin creep. She had never been near water that made absolutely no sound whatsoever. It did not even lap at the shore. She bent and dipped her fingers into it, making sure that it was water and not crystal. When she removed her hand and shook it, the drops fell back into the lake without a splash or even a ripple; they simply rejoined the rest of the water.

Everyone stepped back from the water's edge involuntarily. Even Leaflighter suppressed a shudder. "Queen's magic," she whispered.

The group moved closer together, staring blindly into the swirling, shifting, ghostly mist.

"Are you sure there's an island in there?" Heini asked. His voice sounded impossibly loud and strangely muted at the same time. The group drew closer still.

"Of course I'm sure," Leaflighter said sharply. "And you'd do well to whisper, mortal — we're in the Queen's presence now."

"She knows we're here?" Meryl asked tremulously.

"She knows," Leaflighter replied. "The mist shields her, not us."

"How comforting," Heini muttered. "I can't seem to remember why I decided to come here with you."

"*Hruumph-nha*," sniffed Halstatt.

"That has to be the most cautious sniff he's ever made," thought Meryl. Aloud she said, "Well, we can't just stand here growing roots — no offence, Halstatt. What should we do, Leaflighter?"

The fairy shrugged. "I told you, no one knows what will please the Queen. If she's interested, she'll hear you, and if she isn't, she won't."

"Great," snapped the mabinog. "Well, here we go ..." She took a deep breath.

Halstatt immediately slapped a hand across her mouth. "Prunes and porpoises, what do you think you're doing?" he hissed in her ear.

"I'm going to ask her if we can come to Avalon," Meryl growled back.

"Oh, just like that, are you? 'Ahem. Dear Queen of the Winds, lovely Lady of the Lake, do you mind if we pop over and have a poke about your rose garden?' Is that your plan?" The draoi's voice dripped with sarcasm.

"That's it," Meryl stormed back. "Have you got a better idea?"

The draoi fumed but wouldn't answer. Leaflighter laughed and ran her elegant fingers casually through her tangled hair. Heini stared up into the mist and began to whistle nonchalantly.

"We should wait to see what the Queen will do," the draoi answered finally.

"The King tried that once," Leaflighter said. The others turned to her.

"What happened?" Meryl demanded.

"We sat here until the King's beard grew long, and then she sent a gale that blew us back onto the Way," the fairy replied cheerfully. "It was a great lark of a storm, actually. Much more interesting than just sitting around."

"Forget that," Meryl said decisively. "You all heard what Judge Williams said. If we believe we're right we need to convince the Queen. We can't just sit here hoping she'll invite us to visit her."

Meryl broke away from the group and walked right to the water's edge.

"Hello!" she called. Halstatt groaned behind her. "My name is Meryl, and these are my friends, Heini, Halstatt and Leaflighter. We'd like to come see you, please."

Her voice rolled through the mist and echoed faintly, and then all was silent again.

"How eloquent," muttered the draoi.

"A bit flat," agreed Heini, "but then one hardly knows the best way to address a bank of fog." Meryl turned and glared at him.

The silence stretched out. Then, just as Meryl was about to try again, the earth trembled. It was as though the ground were shaking in silent laughter beneath them. The water of the lake remained undisturbed, but the companions were nearly knocked off their feet. In a panic they clung to one another. Then, a voice like a thousand sighs said, "Come as best you can, if you can." Silence descended again, and the earth was stilled.

"Oh dear," said the draoi.

"Well," Heini said brightly, "at least she didn't say no. That might help your case with the King."

Leaflighter shrugged. "It's a better response than most receive."

"Though a tad enigmatic," the fool added.

"Oh dear, oh dear," moaned the draoi again.

"Oh come on, Halstatt, it's not that bad," Meryl said, hopefully.

"Not that bad? Not that bad! Oh my roots and berries, it's as bad as it can be!"

"Really?" Meryl said. "You think I'll lose my voice?" She felt her throat tighten at the thought, and her stomach lurched once again.

"Lose your voice? Yes, along with the rest of you, if you see what I mean."

"No, I don't." Meryl felt her heart sink to her boots. "Stop speaking in riddles."

"It's a challenge. Now we have to get there on our own, or die in the attempt, or sit here and wait for the King to show up and condemn us to eternal root rot or some equally ghastly fate for failing to obey the Queen's command, indeed, indeed." The draoi sat down and began snapping off his own twiggy fingers in distress.

"Stop that!" Meryl said, yanking him back to his feet. He blinked at her in astonishment. "Now tell me if I understand you correctly. The Queen has just ordered us to try to get to Avalon on our own." The draoi nodded miserably. "And if we don't try, but sit here and wait for the King, he'll punish us for not doing as we've been told?" Halstatt nodded again.

Meryl looked at Heini. Heini looked at the sky and began whistling once more. She looked at Leaflighter. The fairy grinned and shrugged.

"Well, you're all extremely helpful," the mabinog grumbled. She thought furiously for a moment, then asked, "Can we swim to the island?" She didn't add that she'd first have to learn how to swim. Matters seemed complicated enough already.

Leaflighter began to laugh.

Halstatt's eyes nearly fell out of his head. "Swim? Frogs and fleabites, anyone not educated at the fine institution of the Hall knows that the mists of Avalon are woven from the souls of those who've tried to swim there. It's a magical lake, not a bathing pool, *hruumph-nha.*"

"Oh," said Meryl. She stared at the mist with new-found horror. "Well, what about a boat? Is there a magical boat hidden here that can be summoned somehow?"

"The King has tried to find one for centuries, without luck," Leaflighter spluttered, wiping tears of mirth from her eyes.

"I wish you wouldn't find our impending death so humorous," Meryl snapped at her.

"My apologies," she replied, trying to suppress her grin.

Meryl glared at her, then continued racking her brain.

"Leaflighter," she said slowly, "how quickly can you get to the dancing green and back, if you go by yourself?"

"In a wink," the fairy said, puzzled. "But I can't go at all, you know. I have to stay with you."

"No, the King said you had to stay with us until we arrived at the shores of Avalon and heard the Queen's response to our request. You've done that."

"But ..." the fairy began.

"So," Meryl continued, "you could just whip back to the green, find King Iubdan and convince him to lend Halstatt, the fine draoi who found his poor wandering people a new home, those magical shoes of his. Then you bring them back here." She smiled brilliantly at her companions.

Heini whistled one long note, this time in admiration.

"You can't take the fairy King's shoes!" Leaflighter exclaimed indignantly.

"They aren't the fairy King's yet — not until they've finished dancing on the green, and the three days aren't over yet. Besides, we're only going to borrow them to get to Avalon. You can bring them right back when we're done."

"And how eager will King Iubdan be to lend the price of his new home just before the payment is due?" Leaflighter insisted.

"I told you, he's lending them to Halstatt, the saviour of his people. Besides, Halstatt can have a thingy on him that he'll get them back in time."

"I beg your pardon?" the draoi asked stiffly.

"You know, a thingamacallit — a geis, that's what I mean. King Iubdan is sure to accept that."

"Ah yes, a geis. Set a law of fate on myself that I'll turn into a toad, or a stork, or some such divine creature if I don't return them in time, indeed, indeed. Then off to Avalon, where the Queen throws me under a spell of enchanted sleep full of hideous nightmares, from which I wake as a croaking bullfrog a thousand years from now. What a charming plan you've developed."

"Very well, I'll set the geis on me, if you're going to be that way about it. Don't you see, Halstatt, that this could be our only chance?" Meryl looked at the draoi pleadingly.

He glared at her. "Even if we get the shoes, may I remind you that one pair of shoes does not carry four people across the water?"

"I'll carry you across on my back," Meryl replied stoutly. "Then you can go back for Heini, and Heini can go back for Leaflighter, and Leaflighter can go back on her own and bring the shoes back to Iubdan."

"I'm not going to miss out on all the fun," Leaflighter protested.

"Someone has to bring the shoes back to keep Halstatt from being turned into a toad," Meryl argued.

"Ah, I see the geis is back on me, *hruumph-nha*."

"Well, the Faylinn trust you," explained the mabinog.

"I'll try to get the shoes without the geis," Leaflighter said. "There's no way I'm going to miss the fun. The King wouldn't like it," she finished primly.

"Fine, no geis," Meryl said. "But he has to give you the shoes willingly — no tricks or lies, Leaflighter. We don't need any more trouble."

"Of course!" the fairy said. "You can trust me implicitly." And she vanished with a grin.

"What a terrifying thought," Heini said to the air where she'd been standing.

"And I'm not carrying you on my back like some witless donkey," Halstatt said to the fool.

"You'll have to, Halstatt," Meryl argued. "I can't carry him."

"He may carry me, after I go back for him," the draoi replied imperiously. "Draoi are not made to bear burdens. We're a contemplative people, if you see what I mean."

"Very clearly," agreed Heini, and he swept the draoi a bow. "It would be an honour to bear your contemplative weight upon my mulish back, oh great oracle." He then began to dance about, singing:

> I knew an old draoi from the forest
> Subjected to treatment most boorish
> He sat on a fool
> He thought was a mule
> And was thrown on his rump with a flourish.

Meryl laughed and joined in the dancing.

Halstatt began to splutter and hiss. "You'll do no such thing!" he shouted.

"Don't be so sure," Heini shot back.

"Well, I think you're both horrible, I do indeed, indeed," the draoi muttered.

"Oh, stop snivelling, Halstatt." Meryl stopped dancing and patted the draoi's leafy back. "Of course Heini won't toss you into the lake. But you might have asked him to carry you, rather than demanding it, you know."

The draoi glared down at the ground. "Will you carry me?" he finally asked. Meryl was sure he didn't mean to sound as surly as he did.

"Sure, old beansprout!" Heini said, clapping him on the back. The draoi winced, but only muttered "*Hruumph-nha*" once or twice under his breath.

It was then that Leaflighter returned. She held a pair of ridiculously small leather slippers in her hand and flashed one of her infamous grins. "Here are the slippers, procured through honest begging, and with nary a geis in sight," she exclaimed proudly.

Meryl took them from her in horror, holding them up for the others to see.

"We're doomed," Heini said solemnly.

"I agree," Meryl replied.

"Why?" Leaflighter asked, puzzled. "These are the slippers, and King Iubdan assured me that they'll work even with someone being carried on the wearer's back."

"Leaflighter, I can hardly fit them on my thumb, let alone my feet," Meryl wailed.

"Goats and groundhogs, what do they talk about all day in that Hall of yours?" the draoi exclaimed. "The magic slippers of the Faylinn fit the wearer, whoever the wearer might be. Obviously the last person to wear them was one of the Faylinn. Stop gaping at me like a flounder and put them on."

Meryl looked at the shoes doubtfully. "Can I wear them over my boots?" she asked.

"Best not," the fool suggested. "You should have the magic rubbing up against your toes, I should think. Otherwise they might not work properly, or at the very least you'd be too clumsy to carry an oracle on your back."

A perfect comedy act followed. Heini struggled for some time, pulling the mabinog's boots off and nearly tumbling backwards into the enchanted lake while doing so. Then Meryl had to get her boots, travelling pack and staff, which she refused to leave behind on the shore, rigged safely onto Halstatt's back, then a loudly protesting Halstatt rigged safely onto her own back, holding on as tightly as his twigs could manage, and finally the tiny magical shoes placed on her feet by a feeble, laughing fairy while she leaned on the fool.

"Couldn't you have put the shoes on before the draoi?" Heini complained.

"Oh, be quiet, you didn't think of it either," she snapped back.

Finally they were ready. Gingerly, Meryl stepped out onto the water. It felt firm beneath her — just like walking on land. She took a few hesitant steps and then began to mince forward, until Leaflighter called out, "At that rate the King will be here before you've walked a hundred paces."

"Just you wait until it's your turn," she called back. But she did try to walk normally after that.

Meryl discovered very quickly that it was better not to look down when she walked; the sight of the lake bottom far beneath her made her dizzy, as though she were on a cliff. That fear was swallowed up by another all too soon as the mist rose and swirled around them. "Don't think about where it comes from," she told herself. Aloud she said, "I hope it's not far to the island."

"I hope the island's straight ahead," the draoi answered grimly.

Meryl stopped abruptly. "I hadn't thought of that," she said in horror.

"What a surprise — a human who hasn't thought of something. I might die of shock, indeed, indeed, I might," he answered sarcastically.

"Just remember that I didn't promise not to dump you in the lake," Meryl snapped back.

There was silence then, as the mist closed in on them almost menacingly.

"Please don't," Halstatt said quietly.

Meryl realized that he was as terrified as she was. "Oh Halstatt, you know I'd never do that," she assured him. "We're in this together, and whatever happens will happen to us both."

"*Hruumph-nha*," he replied.

She walked on through the mist, hoping that she was going in a straight line, fighting the urge to yell into the silence of the fog surrounding them. Halstatt grew increasingly heavy on her back. Once she stumbled, and for a terror-filled moment fought to regain her balance. After that she walked more slowly.

"How long have we been walking?" she once whispered to Halstatt.

"I don't know," he replied miserably. His answer scared her so much she decided not to ask again.

She walked farther. There was no way to tell direction; no footprints were left on the lake to let them know if she had walked there before. They struggled blindly on, the silence a shroud about them. Meryl began to imagine herself finally sinking in exhaustion under the water, and wondered if it would be painful to drown in a magical lake. Then she thought of herself as one of the lost souls that made up the mist. Her flesh started to creep, and small pearls of sweat broke out on her upper lip. The mists seemed to be taking shape around her; she could hear ghostly voices whispering just at the limit of her hearing. The mists were tugging at her, like spectral hands dragging her to a similiar doom. Halstatt's weight was pressing down on her back. The blood began to thrum in her ears and she felt as though she might faint.

"I'm going to sing," she said desperately, in an effort to distract herself. "If we're going to die in a magical fogbank, I'm going to go out like a real bard."

"Fine," Halstatt said in a quavery voice. "Just don't sing that confounded cat song."

"It's my only completed work," Meryl protested.

"Complete another," the draoi replied firmly.

Meryl felt frustrated, but as she stumbled again she decided the idea was wise. If she were puzzling out a song she wouldn't be able to think as much about their situation.

The mabinog began to hum, until a tune, strange and lilting, took shape. She played with the tune, exploring its cadences and discovering variations. Slowly words began to emerge as well. It was as though she were taking the eeriness of the mist and making it part of herself; embracing it, rather than fighting against it. She became so absorbed that she trudged on, mindless for a time to the danger they were in.

Amid the snows of winter,
Within the world's night,
When hope grew ever dimmer
There bloomed a flower bright.

The darkness it dispelled,
Faint-heartedness it quelled,
And all who saw its burning
Knew peace with them now dwelled.

Halstatt sniffed into Meryl's hair. "My treasure," he muttered.

Oh, come join the fairy band,
Journey to the Summer Land,
Where the Rose of Hope's still blooming
Beyond reach of human hands.

She went back to humming, searching her mind for the next part of the tale, the part clouded in mystery. Why did Taliesin take the rose, and where did he take it?

Suddenly Halstatt's hands clutched about her throat. "Look!" he yelped, pointing to their right.

Meryl turned. At the urging of a gentle wind the mist was parting, and the outline of a shore could be seen. "Thank goodness!" she gasped, increasing her speed. It was a difficult task, with an excited draoi thumping her and exclaiming, "Hurry, hurry," with each step.

"I'd hurry better if you'd stop hitting me," she hissed.

"I beg your pardon," he replied.

It was an island, bathed in sunshine. The trees were in full bloom, their pale-pink blossoms incredibly large and fragrant. Meryl and Halstatt could smell their perfume from the moment they sighted the island. As they got nearer, they saw with amazement that the trees bore ripe fruit at the same time. A lovely scent of green, growing things filled the air, and the welcome song of birds, sweet and incredibly pure, was heard, punctuating the long silence at last. It was with a shock that Meryl realized the birds were whistling her own tune. When Meryl and Halstatt reached the shore at last, they threw themselves upon the land.

"We made it!" Meryl shrieked in delight. If she hadn't been so exhausted she was sure that she'd have been dancing around as delightedly as the draoi.

"Truly surprising," said a musical voice.

They spun in the direction it came from. A young fairy maiden, smaller than Leaflighter and with decidedly green hair — though a very pleasant apple-green, Meryl thought — stepped forward from a path between the trees. She was wearing a long, luminous robe, in the same colour as her hair, which was shimmering so brightly in the sunlight that it was difficult to look directly at her.

"Are you the Queen of the Summer Land?" the mabinog asked, in awe.

The maiden looked shocked. "Certainly not." Then she laughed. "And I'll do you a great favour and not mention to anyone that you asked me that. I'm called Awela. I blow away the mists so that those favoured by the Queen may come unto the island. I bring you greetings, and I shall lead you to our Queen."

"Oh well, thank you," Meryl stuttered. "I mean, thank you very much for blowing away those mists, and all, but you see, we can't go to the Queen just yet."

"Oh? And what keeps you, tempting her wrath?"

"Wrath? Oh, dear. Well, you see, we have two companions on the other shore, and —"

Awela laughed and waved her hand at the lake. "See where your friends come," she said.

And true enough, a small boat, beautiful in its simplicity, drew to the shore. It was fashioned from a golden-coloured wood and built on straight, uncomplicated lines, with no ornate decoration. It glided across the surface of the lake as smoothly as a swan.

Leaflighter, who had been sitting in the bow, grinning, leaped out as soon as they touched land. Heini, also smiling, followed. "That saves me a sore back, doesn't it now?" he said cheerfully to the group.

"What distasteful apparel," Awela replied.

The fool only bowed and said, "Heini Heilin, court fool, at your service, dear lady." He drew his jangling cap out of his pack and donned it once more, to complete the rakish effect.

"A boat," Meryl said in disgust. "That's not fair."

"It took you a good long time to earn your way here," Awela replied. "Once the Queen has made up her mind she doesn't like to be kept waiting. The boat was the quickest solution."

Leaflighter and Awela laughed in unison at the sight of Meryl's disgruntled expression, then stopped and eyed each other carefully.

"A King's servant," said Awela, after some consideration.

"Yes," replied Leaflighter.

"But not a very good one," Meryl added waspishly. "She's always forgetting orders and playing tricks."

"Sounds like a perfect fairy!" Awela laughed in response. "Welcome, red one. Come, the Queen is not to be kept waiting."

"Just a minute," Meryl interrupted.

Awela stopped. "Do you have any more friends you need transported here?" she inquired icily.

"No, but I'd like to put my own boots on, and get my walking staff and pack from Halstatt, if you don't mind."

Awela nodded. With a minimal amount of fuss Meryl was booted, stowed the magical slippers in her pack and had the security of her sturdy staff once again. "Now I'm ready," she said. "That is, as ready as I'll ever be."

They walked along the path through the marvellous apple orchard. All of the trees had smooth bark and straight limbs; there wasn't a single blemish on any leaf, as far as the mabinog could tell. The smell of the flowers and the fruit was so heady in places that Meryl thought she'd faint. She was also suddenly aware of how hungry she had become.

"Is there any chance I could have an apple?" she called out to Awela. "I haven't eaten for some time, and carrying a draoi is hard work."

Awela stopped, then shrugged. "Ask and see," she said.

"But I did ask you ... just now. So ... may I?"

The fairy looked puzzled. "I don't know. They aren't my apples."

"Then whose are they?"

The green fairy laughed in amazement. "Why, the tree's, of course. Who else's? Really, mortal, you do have the strangest ideas."

Meryl looked at Halstatt. "Is this a fairy joke?"

"Of course not," the draoi replied. "The trees in the Summer Land are magical in more ways than one, as anyone with a proper education knows, indeed, indeed. Really, I think that I shall go personally to that ridiculous Hall of yours and examine the Masters myself. It's astonishing, that's what it is, *hruumph-nha.*"

Meryl felt utterly idiotic, but still she walked up to one of the apple trees, cleared her throat and said, "If you please, I'm very hungry, and I'd truly appreciate having one of your apples to eat, if you can spare one."

There was silence, then a rustling in the branches. A perfect apple, russet and sweet-smelling, fell into her hand.

"Thank you," she said. And it seemed that the tree bent its trunk to her.

"Bowing trees," said Meryl. "Now I've seen everything."

"Oh, hardly that," Awela assured her. "But now we must hurry — the Queen awaits."

They trotted along the path, Meryl savouring each bite from her magical apple. The trees thinned, the group came out into the clearing, and everyone, save Awela, gasped. The core fell from Meryl's hand, forgotten.

There is no castle like the castle of the Fairy Queen. It is white and shining and crystalline and spired. Meryl found that she could not look at any part of it directly for very long; it dazzled the eye and could be beheld only in glances. Her gaze fluttered around each wonder of its architecture like a moth around a lantern, alighting only briefly before seeking a new vantage point. She glimpsed a crystal gate beneath a soaring, arched doorway; filigreed spires that rose so high they kissed the clouds; tall windows that glinted like diamonds in the sunlight. Looking at it was like looking at a dance of rainbows. It was beauty itself.

"Come," said Awela. "You are expected."

CHAPTER TWENTY

MERYL AND HER FRIENDS walked along corridors that seemed to have been built of light. The mabinog was sure that there were no shadows in the castle of the Fairy Queen. At last Awela conducted them into an expansive hall with an impossibly high ceiling, a wide, white marble floor, and a row of tall, gleaming windows along either side. Their eyes were dazzled by the brightness of the rainbow fairies moving through the glimmering air. Like the King's servants, each fairy represented a colour, but that was where all similarity ended. The Queen's servants did not move in bands but individually, and when two blue fairies came near one another Meryl saw that they were so different in hue that they could hardly be considered the same colour at all. She no longer thought of Awela as green, but rather saw in her the spirit of all growing things when they first break through the dark soil and bathe in the warm spring sunshine.

She also noticed that Leaflighter appeared decidedly uncomfortable in the crowd. Her colour was like a gash of red paint against the airy tones that swirled about them. She caught Meryl's eye upon her and smiled ruefully. "A riotous lot," she said lightly, but the mabinog noticed that she kept close to her travelling companions.

Meryl's stomach was churning more furiously than ever before, making her regret the apple she'd eaten. "Remember — your quest is worthy, you have a right to be here," she kept telling herself silently. Yet the thought gave her no comfort. Involuntarily her hand clutched at her throat, as though she could already feel her voice being torn from her. The surge of fairies around her gave her the sensation of being caught in a whirlpool of colour; she fought to pull air into her lungs with ragged gasps. A splinter of memory flashed through her brain, jarred loose by the shimmering shades around her. She saw the soap bubbles shining on the floor she'd just finished washing in Derwena's humble cottage. It seemed a beautiful haven to her now, rather than the dull prison she had thought it then. The Mistress's prediction that her quest would leave her either a bard, or broken, or dead, rose unbidden to her mind. In her panic she thought that the last option might even be the most preferable.

"Awela," Meryl choked out, "where's the Queen?"

The fairy threw her a mocking glance. "You'll know her well enough when you see her," she replied.

It was then that all motion in the room ceased. The Queen's servants formed two long rows on either side of the hall, as though they were lining up for a dance. At the end of the hall stood a single, tall throne, elegantly carved from the same white marble that was used for the floor. It had been obscured by the fairies but was now clearly visible. Before it stood the Queen.

Awela was quite correct; there could be no mistaking her. Her robe appeared to be woven of refracted light, while her long white hair glimmered and sparkled with radiance, cascading down to her feet. Looking at her made Meryl feel as though she were seeing the very heart of a star. She didn't even realize that she had fallen to her knees until the Queen spoke. Once again the group heard that sighing voice, but this time Meryl recognized its power of command.

"Rise, and come forward," said the Queen. The mabinog found herself obeying, though she didn't feel as though it were possible to move.

The group stopped several feet before the throne, huddled together as though they were one body.

"Which is the one who requested admittance to my presence?" asked the Queen. Meryl felt herself jostled forward.

"I am ... I mean, I did, Your Majesty," she stammered. She remembered her bellowed request on the other shore of the lake, and writhed in humiliation.

"And so you are ... Meryl?" the Queen continued, seeming to wonder at the strangeness of the mortal name.

"Ah, yes, that's right, Your Majesty. I'm a mabinog, you see, and I'm on a quest." She stopped short and caught her breath. There was no turning back now.

"A mabinog," said the Queen. She paused, then sat down upon her throne. "A mabinog on a quest, no less. Awela, how long has it been since a mabinog from the Hall quested at our shores?"

"Well over a century, Great Queen, and well over two centuries since the last one was admitted, though we have had a few wandering minstrels since that time."

"I had thought the world had tired of mabinogs, or that they had tired of questing. I wondered if the world had any bards left in it."

"Oh, plenty," answered Meryl. Halstatt snorted. "It's just that they stay at the Hall now, and mabinogs learn by studying from the Masters."

"But not you," said the Queen.

"No," replied Meryl. "Not me."

Silence descended as the Queen studied the group. Finally she spoke again, this time to Leaflighter.

"King's servant."

"Yes, my lady Queen?"

"Why are you here, with this mortal band?"

"By the King's orders, my lady Queen."

"Oh?" The Queen leaned forward, with interest.

"This mortal and this fern-friend are to be placed under your judgement, O Queen."

Meryl felt Halstatt creep next to her. Furtively she reached down and clasped his hand. In the midst of her terror she noticed that he had several new twiggy stumps growing back where his fingers had been broken off.

"Why are they sent to be judged by me? Can the King not reason for himself?" the Queen asked with a smile. Laughter rippled through her servants, then all was quiet again.

"Of course, my lady Queen. But their case was an unusual one. You see, this mortal brought iron on our Way."

A murmur followed, like the murmur of the sea.

"Iron on the Way? Why did the King not curse them and be done with it?" The Queen looked with distaste at the mabinog, then noticed her clasp. Her frown deepened. Meryl felt her knees begin to shake.

"Her story caught the King's interest. She claimed to be journeying to the Summer Land to learn the story of a magical rose that bloomed even in winter, a rose that this tree-twin says he possessed for a time. It was supposedly stolen from him by the bard Taliesin, who once had the joy of meeting you, my lady. They thought that the rose came from here, and may, perchance, have been returned. The King grew curious too, my lady, and decided that if you would hear them, they would not be cursed." Leaflighter bowed as she finished speaking. Meryl briefly wondered if the fairy had ever been so polite in her life.

"A rose that bloomed in winter," said the Queen slowly. "The rose of the Eastern King." A sigh went up from the fairy host. The Queen stood. "Come with me," she said.

She led the companions out a small door, followed by a solemn train of twelve fairy courtiers. In a silent parade they moved from the hall out into a most exquisite garden. Once again

Meryl thought she heard the distant sound of birds warbling her mist-tune, but when she strained her ears to make sure, the song faded away.

They walked along a pathway bordered by flowers both like and unlike any Meryl had ever seen. Their shapes and colours and scents were the same as the familiar flowers of Albaine, but intensified a hundred times. It was as though all the flowers of the mortal world were no more than the shadows of the real blooms that lived in Avalon. Indeed, Meryl soon suspected that these flowers were living in the same manner as were the trees of the Summer Land. Though there was no breeze, all the blossoms bent their heads to the Queen as she passed by. Meryl slowed slightly to inspect a daisy for signs of life, and she was sure she saw it wink at her encouragingly before Heini pushed her firmly on from behind.

Her pulse began to throb wildly in expectation. It seemed obvious that a magical rose such as Halstatt's would be found in this place. Yet somehow, even with the stately pace of the procession making the moment so solemn, she couldn't help but feel incredulous that she was about to find the object of her quest almost immediately after arriving in Avalon. She was convinced that she was merely a heartbeat away from the answer to the riddle of Taliesin's theft, yet each majestic footstep grated on her jangling nerves. A part of her shrank with misgiving. Was her quest for the rose to end so abruptly? Could she really be so close to her goal?

At last they came to the centre of the garden. There was a bed of earth, bordered by stones — but nothing grew there. On this island of endless growing life the bareness struck like a blow. It was the island's scar.

"Here is where the Eastern King's rose bloomed, for many a century," said the Queen, gazing down at the bare earth in sorrow. "A traveller came here, long ago, weary and sore from his journey. He came from distant eastern lands with a message of hope for all human people. He told of a King who wore a crown of thorns, and because he wore it out of love the blood of his brow blossomed into roses on the thorn. The traveller had a staff made from the thorn tree — much like yours, in fact," the Queen said to Meryl.

"Mine was made for me by a friend," Meryl offered. "He told me he'd heard of one like it in a tale."

The Queen nodded, and continued. "The traveller leaned upon it, here in my garden, and it, too, blossomed as he told his tale. Here I kept it until an old draoi of Eire came to my shores."

There was a gasp from Halstatt. "I believe that was ... my mother," he stammered.

"Indeed?" replied the Queen. "I found her a most delightful creature. She begged to see the flower, and when she had seen it she fell down and wept for three days. It was a most unusual sight."

"And then?" prompted Meryl.

"And then she begged me to allow her to take the rose back to the world of mortals, where it could once again bring inspiration during the times of darkness. I was loath to let it go, but I felt it was as the Eastern King would have wished. He was ever sympathetic to the plight of mortals." The Queen sounded amused at the thought.

Meryl picked up the story. "And so the rose was passed to Halstatt from his mother, and then Taliesin, we believe, stole it — and we're no closer to discovering its whereabouts now."

She felt defeated. It took all her will to fight back the tears stinging her eyes. She had been so sure, after hearing that Taliesin had been to the Summer Land, that he had brought the rose back to Avalon. Dejectedly she stared at the piece of barren earth, and to her horror some tears did spill down her cheeks. Though she dashed them away with her hand, she knew that everyone had seen them. She tried to smile at the draoi, but it twisted into a grimace.

"Oh well," she said, too loudly and with false gaiety.

"Cheer up," said Heini. "Perhaps your rose has had adventures of its own and is waiting for you somewhere back in Albaine!"

"Maybe another fortunate draoi now has the honour of tending it," muttered Halstatt, wistfully.

"Wherever it is, you'll find it," added Heini, confidence strengthening his words. "This journey to Avalon wasn't a failure — at least you've learned the story of the rose. That has to count for a great deal."

"Besides," Leaflighter added wickedly, "there's also that matter of the cauldron to deal with." She grinned at Meryl, who glared back at her, to no effect.

"The cauldron?" A knowing look crossed the Queen's face. "That would be the cauldron of Ceridwen?"

"That's right," answered Meryl, her face flaming.

"Ah, the mabinog wishes to become a bard."

"Well, that is the purpose of every mabinog's quest," Meryl replied defensively.

"Indeed," answered the Queen. "Yet you know the dangers of the cauldron?"

"Yes."

"And still you wish to drink from it?"

Meryl was silent. She felt all eyes upon her. "I'm not sure any more," she finally replied.

"I see," said the Queen. "Well, time brings no pressures in my land. Now that you are here you are welcome to stay a while. You will rest, and enjoy the land, and tell me stories of your journey, and then you will decide. Yes?"

Meryl looked at her companions. They all nodded enthusiastically, even Halstatt.

"Yes," she agreed.

Her only comfort was the realization that she'd probably keep her voice.

Chapter Twenty-One

THE FOLLOWING DAYS were filled with countless pleasures. The Queen's court delighted in the novelty of having guests and seemed willing to go to any effort to make the visitors happy and comfortable. Even Halstatt's opinion of fairies improved, while Heini and Leaflighter were always laughing.

In those days it was Meryl alone who was troubled. The Queen had shown her where Ceridwen's cauldron was kept, in a room atop a high tower. Meryl went there by herself, several times a day, but each time she turned away, its magic untested.

The cauldron was small, no larger than Tanwen's big kettle. It was a thing of beauty, wrought of three shades of thin gold that twisted and spiralled in intricate patterns, with large pearls set about its rim. Standing on a lone pedestal, in the centre of the empty tower room, it contained what Meryl supposed was a magical wine, a clear, ruby liquid that gave off a delicious scent when you stood near it. Four large windows, one in each wall, looked out on the world in all directions and they filled the room with the heady light that flooded all of Avalon during the day. The cauldron sparkled in the sunshine and seemed to entreat Meryl to try its magic, but every time she reached for it, the horror of madness would fill her, and her hand would fall back to her side.

On the fourth day of their visit, as Meryl stood in the tower, she chanced to look out one of the windows and was greeted with the sight of the King's court on the far shore of the enchanted lake. With a start of dismay she remembered the magical slippers, still in her pack. She tore down the hundred steps from the tower, then raced into the Queen's hall.

The court was being entertained by Heini. The fairies delighted in all his riddles and tumbling routines; Heini claimed that he'd never had a more appreciative audience in his life. He looked a bit put out, therefore, when Meryl came dashing through the hall, spoiling one of his best conundrums.

"The King! The King is here, Your Majesty!" Meryl yelped.

"On the island?" the Queen exclaimed, rising from her throne.

"No, no, I mean on the shore, the other shore," Meryl panted.

"Ah!" The Queen, seated herself again, calmly. "It has been a while since he last came to call."

"But you see, your Majesty, I forgot about the shoes I'd borrowed. They're his now, and I was supposed to return them to King Iubdan before they were to be given as payment. I might have wrecked the bargain between the Twlwyth Teg and the Faylinn, and —"

The Queen cut her off. "Set your heart at rest. The bargain has been kept. The Faylinn occupy their new homeland, and the King ..." She paused for a moment. "The King did rage indeed, for he wanted those shoes for the same purpose as you, much good they would have done him." She smiled sweetly as she looked at the girl. "He should have known that there is no way onto my island, magical or otherwise, save by my own permission. I would have been content to let him wander in the mist for a thousand years," she added. The court laughed delightedly.

Meryl was hardly reassured, however. The King's rage was what she was trying to avoid, not arouse, and she said as much to the Queen.

"Leave the King's rage to me," replied the Queen. "I'm well used to dealing with it." The court laughed again.

"Still, I made a bargain," Meryl insisted. "May I send Leaflighter back with the shoes?"

"Why me?" yelped the fairy. "I said I didn't want to miss the fun!"

"Well, you haven't," Meryl snapped back. "You got to see Avalon, and you witnessed the Queen listening to our request, so now you can bring the shoes back to the King and tell him not to curse us."

"You still haven't decided on the cauldron," Leaflighter pouted. "I think I should wait until you've made up your mind about that. The King will want to know."

Meryl opened her mouth to argue, but the Queen cut her short. "King's servant," she said kindly, "we have found you a most entertaining guest, and we would be sorry to lose your company. However, the human is right. A bargain made should be a bargain kept."

Leaflighter began to protest, but the Queen continued. "I shall send you in my boat with the shoes. You shall convey them to the King, with this message from me: the human and the draoi have been heard, and I judge their quest sufficiently worthy to absolve them of their crime. Then," and here the Queen's eyes sparkled with mischief, "I command you to return, that I might have news of his reaction, and that you might bear any message of his to me. Only you alone may return in the boat; otherwise it shall vanish into the mist. Understood?"

Leaflighter crowed with delight. Meryl ran and got her the slippers, which the fairy took from her gleefully. "I can't wait to see how jealous they'll all be when I get to come back here a second time!" she laughed. She left with Awela for the shore, and Meryl was sure that she skipped the entire way.

The fairy was gone some time, and Meryl grew tired of waiting. Heini's riddles irritated her, and even the music of fairy laughter began to grate on her nerves. Briefly she considered going back to the tower room, but the warmth of the afternoon made her drowsy, and the thought of those hundred stairs daunted her. So she strolled into the Queen's garden instead.

Soon she found herself at the garden's centre, staring at the empty flower bed. She knelt down beside it and ran her fingers through the earth. "I wonder where you are," she muttered to herself. "Where would Taliesin take you?"

As she sat in silence her thoughts went back to the beginning of her quest. "What would you say to me now, Mistress Derwena?" she asked aloud. "I've come all this way, and the cauldron is in my reach. Would you tell me to drink from it, or not?"

Silence answered her. Meryl found herself suddenly filled with homesickness for the Hall, and for the wise and patient kindness of the Woodcrone. She thought about that other garden, with its patch of marigolds, and smiled as she compared it to the lush beauty surrounding her now. From her small coin purse she took the old rose sprig. It was so brittle she was afraid it would turn to powder in her hand. She looked at it critically.

"You're hardly an inspiration," she said to the sprig. In a fit of pique she stuck it into the earth, at the centre of the empty flower bed. It was just a dry twig poking out of the soil. Meryl laughed at the sight.

A shout came from the castle. Meryl recognized Heini's voice. "Leaflighter must have returned!" she exclaimed, and she ran back to the hall.

There, the fairy was bubbling over with delight in her mission. She was in the midst of relaying what sounded like a long speech to the Queen when Halstatt appeared at the mabinog's side and gripped her arm. "We're definitely not going to be cursed!" he hissed excitedly into her ear.

"Are you certain? Even though we kept the shoes too long?" Meryl whispered back.

"Of course I'm certain. I wouldn't have said it if I weren't certain. We draoi value the truth, you know."

"So do humans," Meryl retorted.

"*Hruumph-nha!*"

"Well, most of us do. And there are more of us than there are of you, so there's a greater chance for some to turn out badly."

"Seems like a poor excuse to me," the draoi sniffed. "The quantity of a species doesn't make up for its quality, if you see what I mean."

"*Hruumph-nha*," snorted Meryl.

The draoi looked at her in amazement. "I believe that's the most intelligent thing you've ever said."

For a brief moment Meryl considered hitting him. Then she thought better of it.

It sounded as though Leaflighter wasn't going to finish her speech any time soon. The entire court was taking great delight in the King's latest petition to the Queen, and the laughter of the fairies was both loud and merry. Meryl felt restless again, and left to find a quiet place to think.

This time she rambled about the island, finding peace among the trees. She paused next to an ancient apple tree. "If you were a human, and wanted to be a bard, would you drink from the cauldron of Ceridwen?" she asked.

There was a rustle in the tree's leaves, then came a voice that sounded like boughs creaking in a high wind. "The real question is, will you?"

Meryl strove valiantly to hide her surprise. She knew that the trees of Avalon were uniquely alive, but she had no idea they could actually speak.

"But I can't decide," she said to the tree. "I've gone up to the tower more times than I care to count, but I still can't make up my mind."

"And why is that?" the voice creaked again.

"I'm afraid of going mad."

"Really?"

Meryl became indignant. "Well, it makes sense, doesn't it? Who wants to be mad?"

"Who wants to be a bard?" creaked the apple tree.

"I do, of course," Meryl replied. The tree was silent. "Well, haven't you anything else to say?"

The leaves rustled again, but the tree said nothing further. "I can't say you've been very helpful," Meryl snapped. And with that she marched off towards the shore.

From there she could look across to the King's court. She waved politely, but there was no response or acknowledgment. Then she remembered that while she could see them clearly, they were very likely staring into a fogbank. They seemed to be waiting expectantly. Meryl thought of the long speech Leaflighter was giving, and the laughter of the Queen and her court. "Good luck," she muttered. "I hope you don't have to wait another three hundred years for your answer."

She wandered back to the castle and found herself once again climbing the tower stairs. Soon she was back in the room, hot and tired from her exertions. She looked at the cauldron. "Right now I almost wish you were a regular cauldron holding plain water," she puffed, wiping her brow on her sleeve. Silence settled in the room.

Meryl sat and let her mind wander. She thought again about the tree's question: Did she really want to be a bard? In truth, it was all she had ever wanted. She leaned back against the wall and stared up at the ceiling, remembering the night, only a month after her training at the Hall had begun, when her mother had been named Chief Bard. Meryl had been only seven, like the other new mabinogs, and the treat of staying up late had been both thrilling and bewildering. She had huddled next to her new friend Finian, sharing her warm cloak with him as they sat under the trees and watched the circle of Masters standing around the great bonfire. To Meryl they looked like unlit candles, waiting for the fire to ignite them with a flame of their own. They stood silently and still, the hoods of their long cloaks drawn over their heads to shield their faces. Meryl was unable to tell them apart, though she had known them all her entire life. Even her mother was unknown to her. The sudden strangeness of the familiar figures, the majesty of the roaring fire in the chill autumn night air and the haunting song they began to sing combined to form a vivid memory.

As she sat in the tower room, the words and melody of the song came to her own lips. She began to sing, the bardic flames still burning in her mind.

O, I shall speak with words of fire
I hold the gift to all inspire
I dwell within the rock, alive
I bring the truth, that all may thrive

I am the wood, I am the sun
I am the sea, in all freedom
I am the sky, the birth of stars
I comfort near, and journey far

I carry hope, I promise love
I bear the light from up above
I stand in strength, I sing wisdom
I am the source of all vision

Meryl felt herself held between the power of her memory and the pressure of her choice, as though she were living in two times at once. She felt again the eerie stillness of the night when the Masters had finished singing and no one had dared even to breathe; it seemed they were waiting for a reply. Then, on a whisper of wind, had come her mother's name: "Rhoslyn." Young as she was then, Meryl had felt the small hairs on the back of her neck rise. She knew that they had heard the land speak; it had named their new Chief.

One of the figures stepped into the circle and lowered her hood. Meryl stared at her mother, now the Chief Bard, with mingled pride and awe. She looked so noble and courageous. She had been called to one of the greatest responsibilities in the land, and she was not afraid.

The grip of the memory loosened, and Meryl felt herself caught again by her predicament. She stared at the cauldron before her, remembering her mother's strength and her long-ago promise that she, too, would one day hear the voice of the land. Resolutely she stood.

"The truth is, if I don't drink from you I'll spend the rest of my life wondering what might have been," she said. She stepped nearer. "Wouldn't a life of regret be worse than a life of madness?" She took another step towards the cauldron. "I didn't go on a quest to turn away at the last moment. I am going to be a bard, like my mother before me, like Taliesin before her."

Then she stepped up to the pedestal, placed her hands on the cauldron, and lifted it. Its weight made her gasp, but she didn't falter. She brought its brim up to her mouth, the scent of its contents flooding her senses and making her dizzy.

"Oh dear, I'm going mad already," she thought to herself. Then she drank.

The wine burned on its journey down into her stomach. She waited for something to happen. Cautiously she set the cauldron back down, walked to the west window and sank down on the tower floor. Her head swam.

"I hope I don't make an idiot out of myself once I go crazy," she muttered miserably.

She sat there for some time. The heat of the day wrapped itself around her like a blanket. At one point she even dozed, though for how long she could not tell. Finally she stood up.

"My name is Meryl," she said in a clear voice. Hope filled her. She didn't seem to be crazy; then again, she didn't feel any different, either. She left the tower and crept down to her room.

Once there she pulled out her harp and began to play. She hadn't practised for some days now, and her fingers stumbled. She frowned; fear gripped her. She tried reciting a poem she'd been working on, but she still got stuck in the same place, and no inspiration came. Dread began to blossom in her heart. "My name is Meryl," she repeated. "I'm a questing mabinog."

"I know that," said Heini, from the doorway. He was staring at her curiously. "Or were you talking to the tree outside your window?"

Meryl ignored his question, and fought a rising panic. "Why aren't you in the hall?" she asked.

He shrugged, then came to sit next to her on the bed. "Leaflighter was still talking. I think the King plans to bore the Queen into submission this time. It didn't seem like there was any end in sight."

"Ah," said Meryl. She bit her lip.

Heini looked at her closely, this time with concern. "Are you all right?" he asked.

"Of course I'm all right! Why shouldn't I be all right? Am I acting like I'm not all right?" Her voice rose hysterically, and she struggled to control it.

He stared at her in amazement. Then a strange expression crossed his face. "Did you drink from that cauldron?" he whispered.

For a moment she thought she'd say no; then she remembered telling Halstatt that humans valued the truth. She nodded, miserably.

Heini puffed out a sigh. "And?" he asked gently.

"Well, do I look crazy?" Meryl demanded.

He peered at her, then shook his head. "You look upset, but I wouldn't call you crazy; at least, not more than usual. And after all, I'm an expert on the subject," he quipped with a grin.

Meryl groaned, and lay on her back.

"I'm sorry!" he gasped. "I didn't mean it, really! Stupid joke, that's all. It's the sort of thing that earned me a beating from Coel. You can beat me too, if it'll make you feel better," he pleaded earnestly.

Meryl sat back up, smiling wanly. "Don't be ridiculous," she said.

There was a pause. "Have you tried, ah, barding yet?" he asked tentatively.

Meryl nodded. "My playing is as weak as it ever was, and I still don't know how to finish my poem."

Heini frowned. "Maybe you drank from the wrong cauldron?"

She shook her head dismally. "It was the right one."

"It might take some time to take effect," Heini said then.

"That doesn't sound very magical."

"Well, there's only one thing to do," the fool said resolutely. "We'll go ask the Queen."

Meryl shrank back. "I'd rather not!"

"Come on. You've already done the deed. You might as well know the truth." He pulled her to her feet. "Ready?"

She fought back terror, then nodded. He led her to the hall.

CHAPTER TWENTY-TWO

IN THE HALL, Leaflighter was still speaking and the court was still laughing. When Meryl and Heini arrived, they paused in the doorway, and looked doubtfully at one another.

"What should we do?" Meryl whispered to the fool. "I don't think much of the idea of interrupting the King's message."

"I have to agree with you," he whispered back.

They stood there, at the periphery of the crowd, for some minutes. Then the Queen happened to glance in their direction. She was laughing over some part of the King's message, but when her gaze fell upon Meryl her merriment died abruptly. A strange look came over her face. She stood. At once Leaflighter stopped talking, and the laughter in the hall died.

"Come forward," she said to Meryl.

Head spinning, knees knocking together, Meryl did as she was told. The eyes of everyone in the room were upon her. It was as though she were in a hall of statues, so silent and still were the fairies.

The Queen looked intently into her eyes. "Well?" she asked. The word sounded in Meryl's ears like a clap of thunder, and she winced.

"I ... I took a drink from the cauldron, Your Majesty," she whispered.

The silence deepened.

Meryl shifted her weight nervously from leg to leg. "When does the magic take effect?" she asked.

"The magic of the cauldron of Ceridwen takes effect instantaneously," the Queen replied.

Meryl felt herself fighting to hold back tears. "But it didn't work," she muttered miserably.

"Didn't work?"

"I don't seem to be mad, but when I tried to play my harp I was no better than I was before, and ..." Her voice trailed off. She wished that she had never come to Avalon.

"Ah," said the Queen. "It is not that the magic did not work, mortal, but that you do not understand its working." Meryl looked up at the Queen, hope and fear warring once again in her spirit.

"The magic of the cauldron is simpler than you humans think, but it is also far more powerful. It is not the magic of transformation, changing you into something you were not. It is the magic of revelation. If you are a bard, all is well. If you are not, it reveals you as the madman you are for desiring such a calling."

Meryl wondered if she would ever stop feeling dizzy. "I don't understand," she said. "Why would I be mad for wanting to be a bard?"

There was a ripple of laughter among the fairy host.

The Queen smiled, and looked at Meryl almost pityingly. "To be a bard is to be the servant of all: of Art, of gods and of all people. To be a bard is to roam life's years, calling no place home, telling everyone else's story before your own. To be a bard is to commit yourself to a life of learning, and most learning is achieved through suffering. Only a madman would desire this over the comforts of hearth and home and family, if she were not called to such a life."

The Queen's words swirled around her. The memory of Derwena loomed in her mind, saying that the Hall would never be home to her. She recalled the room she had shared with her mother, now lost to her. She remembered how sore her feet became after a long march, the misery she felt in sleeping outdoors during a rainstorm, and the hunger that gnawed in her belly when she'd eaten nothing but berries for days. Then she recalled the shame of her first performance. Her shoulders slumped.

"I see what you mean," she whispered. Tears welled over her eyelids. She turned away from the Queen.

"Stop, child," came the Queen's command. Meryl halted, but could not look up. "It is hard, the cauldron's magic. Truth is often so. Yet the fact remains, mortal, that you are not mad."

Meryl looked up.

"You are not mad. You are a bard. A young bard, it is true. A good bard? That is still unknown. But your calling is clear. Follow it and see where it leads you." The Queen smiled then, and Meryl felt as though the sun had come out after an entire winter of greyness.

There was a whoop from the crowd, and Meryl found herself crushed between the hugs of Heini and Leaflighter. The fairy host came back to life, and laughter filled the hall once more.

"I need to go outside and get some air," Meryl gasped. "I need to think about all this."

"A most sensible and draoi-like course of action," said Halstatt, appearing on her left. "Clearly your time under my supervision has been beneficial. I suggest a stroll about the garden."

Meryl agreed at once to the suggestion and soon found herself outside, flanked by Heini and Halstatt. Leaflighter remained behind to continue with her speech.

The garden was as lovely as ever, and the scents of the flowers contributed to Meryl's sense of exultation and confusion.

"Let's go have a seat by the rose bed," she suggested. "I need to sit down, I think."

The perfume in the air became heavier as they approached the centre of the garden. Halstatt, perplexed, began to sniff.

"Something else must have bloomed," Heini said.

Halstatt sniffed again. "It smells like ..." He stopped. The draoi and the fool stared at one another, then both broke into a run.

"What is it?" Meryl cried, running after them.

"Can't you tell?" Heini bellowed back at her.

"Tell what?"

They all burst into the centre. Three mouths gaped in astonishment.

A rosebush, small, but laden with glorious red blooms, grew in the once-empty flower bed.

"Impossible," said Heini.

"It's my treasure," said Halstatt. He fell to his knees and touched a petal reverently.

"Are you sure?" Meryl asked the draoi. "It could be an ordinary rose —"

"Of course I'm sure," the draoi snapped. "There is no other rose like it."

Meryl had to agree that it was the most beautiful flower she'd ever seen. Its scent filled the air and seemed to take all her weariness from her. Looking at it, it was impossible not to feel hopeful.

"But how did it get here?" Meryl asked. "Did Leaflighter bring it with her?"

"No," Heini replied, "I was there when she landed on the shore, and she certainly didn't have a rosebush with her. Besides, I'm sure the Queen would have said something if it had been brought back."

"Then how —?" Meryl began again, then stopped. "I wonder ..."

"What?" prompted Heini.

Meryl quickly opened her coin purse. The sprig wasn't there, and she was sure that she had left it in the earth. She looked doubtfully at the plant in luxuriant bloom before her.

"What is it?" Heini asked again.

The blood began to sing in Meryl's ears. "I can't believe it," she whispered. "I had it with me all the time."

Halstatt leapt to his feet. "Had it with you? *Had it with you?* My treasure, my joy ... and you had it with you? I left my lovely moss patch, tramped about all of creation like some lumbering mortal, and now you say —"

"Be quiet, Halstatt," Meryl said calmly. The draoi looked as though he were about to explode. "I didn't know I had it. Just listen." She paused, trying to sort out her thoughts, as understanding dawned upon her.

"At the Hall there was a rosebush — Taliesin's rosebush."

Halstatt began to emit a high-pitched wail. Heini and Meryl glared at him, and he stopped.

"It wasn't magical. I lived there all my life, and it never once bloomed in winter. Nor were there any stories about it doing so, as far as I know. All I was told was that it belonged to Taliesin, and that he always took a bloom with him when he went on a quest, and buried it again at the base of the bush when he returned. It was his inspiration."

"His stolen inspiration!" snapped Halstatt.

"I guess so," Meryl agreed. "He probably knew that it was the rose of the Eastern King, since he'd been to Avalon, and he felt that it should be with mortals, rather than alone in the forest with a draoi."

"Well, he might have asked, *hruumph-nha,*" Halstatt replied waspishly.

"Would you have given it to him?" Heini asked.

The draoi looked offended. "Certainly not, it was a gift from my mother."

"She meant it for people, and so did the Eastern King, the Queen said," Heini argued.

Halstatt glared in reply. "And so it was — for any people who made the effort to come and see me."

"Hardly convenient for the people," Heini shot back.

"Who said it had to be convenient, *hruumph-nha*?" the draoi replied.

Heini was about to respond, but Meryl interrupted. "There's something in that. I don't know if it was because it was stolen, or because it was taken from the wild and sheltered like any normal, tame rose, but it lost its magic at the Hall."

"No, its magic slept," said a voice from behind them.

They turned and found themselves staring at a small brown fairy, as old and wizened as a dried apple or an ancient tree.

"I am Collen," he said, "the Queen's gardener."

He stepped between the companions, touched the bush gently and spoke to it. "Welcome back, old friend." It seemed to Meryl that the leaves shivered in response.

Collen turned to Meryl. "So, you're the mortal that carried iron on the Way?"

Meryl nodded, somewhat surprised. Nobody had referred to that for a while.

"Well, now you know how you did it," he said with a wheezing laugh.

"Larks and lake trout, of course!" Halstatt cried.

"Perhaps you could explain to us mortals," Heini said dryly.

"It's perfectly simple," the draoi announced. "I never arrived at a satisfactory answer to how any mortal, let alone a mortal wearing iron, was able to get on the Way without magical assistance. Every magical being thought that it just couldn't be done. But now we see that she had magical assistance all the time, indeed, indeed."

"The sprig?" said Meryl.

"Of course the sprig! Try to pay attention. The magic of the Way woke up the magic of the sprig, and it asked to come home.

Of course the Way would be only too happy to oblige, mortal or no mortal, iron or no iron. It all makes perfect sense, indeed, indeed it does," he concluded, beaming.

"Quite so," said Collen.

"I had it all the time," Meryl said. Then she began to laugh. "I came for a rose that I had in my pouch, and for a cauldron that told me I've been a bard all along. This has to be the silliest quest ever."

"*Hruumph-nha.* Spoken like a true mortal," snorted Halstatt. "It shouldn't take a draoi to tell you that the purpose of any quest is what you learn along the way, not what you receive at the end."

"You say that now, when you have your rose back," Meryl replied.

The draoi's sudden annoyance faded quickly into sadness. "In point of fact, I do not have my rose back. Avalon has my rose back, if you see what I mean." He looked hopefully at Collen.

The fairy just shook his head. "Not my rose, if you please. The rose of the Eastern King. Its beauty is a gift to all, as is its magic. We shall let the Queen decide its fate."

"No, I've a better idea," Meryl offered.

"I beg your pardon?" Collen was somewhat taken aback.

Meryl smiled. "It seems there are two roses now — one for Avalon, to be kept in trust as the original was, and Taliesin's. There can be no doubt now that he did take it from Halstatt. Good though his intentions probably were, he shouldn't have done it. It was meant to be a light for all people, but it obviously wasn't meant to be found without effort or cost. I think the rose at the Hall must go back to Halstatt, so that he can tend it again and answer the questions of all the mabinogs who I hope will come to see it," she added, grinning at the draoi.

The smile that was stretching across Halstatt's leafy face froze. "Are you saying that I'm to be bothered by more ignorant students of that Hall of yours?" he demanded.

"That's exactly what I'm saying," Meryl replied. "Taliesin's fault seems to be that he helped people too much. He founded the Hall, he brought the rose to the mabinogs, he tried to give them inspiration. He made everything too easy for them, and they grew weak. I think a bard is only meant to direct people towards the path of knowledge; they need to find it for themselves."

The draoi regarded her closely. "I'm astounded," he finally said.

"At what?"

"You've begun truly to think," he answered. "I must admit, there were many times on this journey I didn't believe that would ever happen, indeed, indeed. Well, if the price of my treasure is to have my solitude interrupted by the likes of such as yourself, I think I can probably bear it, *hruumph-nha.*"

"How noble of you," Meryl said. She and the draoi smiled at one another.

Meryl and Heini left Halstatt talking to Collen and wandered back to the castle. Leaflighter was *still* speaking. They looked at one another, then silently turned and walked down to the shore.

"What do I do now?" Meryl asked at last, staring blankly at the still water of the lake.

"I thought you were going back to the Hall for the rose."

Meryl twitched her shoulders restlessly. "I will, but not right away. I'm not ready to go back there yet, and since Halstatt's waited this long, I think he can wait a bit longer."

"All right. Then be a bard," Heini replied.

"But where do I go?"

"Wherever you think you should, I guess."

"You're not being very helpful," Meryl said reproachfully.

"What do you expect? You started out on a quest to become a bard. Now it seems that you can't *become* a bard; you either are one, or you are not. Since you are, work at becoming a good bard. You told the judge that Taliesin spent his life learning after he drank from the cauldron. Don't you still want to be like him?"

"Yes, in a way," Meryl said after a moment. "No matter what mistakes he made, he was the greatest bard ever. I'm proud to use his harp. I'm proud to share his vision. But I'll find my own adventures and sing my own songs. I think that's what I'm meant to do." She paused, then looked at Heini helplessly. "I'm just not sure where to begin."

"I told you, wherever you think you should. Something will come up. Things always do."

"But I had a goal before — Avalon."

"You found that goal when you found Halstatt. You'll find another."

Meryl was silent a moment. "Maybe I should go to the ocean now. I told myself that I would eventually, after I'd gained some experience." She thought of the magical lake and shivered; water still didn't appeal to her.

Heini grinned at her. "Have you ever considered investigating life at Coel's court?"

Meryl looked at him, then grinned back. "I guess it's about time I tried another public performance."

As they walked back to the castle, Meryl thought back on all the adventures her quest had brought her. For the first time since her mother's death, her spirits were high and her heart was full of joy. Was her new happiness the magic gift of the rose, she wondered, or the glad gift of her new friends? It was both, she decided, and as she walked she began to hum the first lines of the song she would call "The Rose of the Eastern King."

EPILOGUE

I T WAS FIVE YEARS LATER, the year of the comet, when the Hall's storytime was interrupted by the arrival of a stranger. A side door was opened, letting in a blast of frigid air and a flurry of snowflakes. Rhydian stopped his telling of "The Most Tragic Tale of the Drowned Maiden" and frowned. No one ever disturbed the doings of the Hall.

A tall figure, well bundled in a woollen cloak and supported by an elaborately carved walking staff, strode up to the hearth, threw back the cloak's hood to reveal a head of cropped, rust-coloured hair, and said clearly, "I've been dreaming of this fire for the past week."

Master Storyteller Rhydian decided to take matters in hand. "This is the Hall, and you have interrupted our tale. I'm sure that if you go to the kitchen they will offer you some warmth and shelter for the night."

"I'm sure they will, Rhydian, and with better grace than you," the stranger remarked with a laugh.

The Master Storyteller stepped back in shock; it had been some time since anyone had spoken to him in such a manner. And the person who did so didn't seem the least bit aware of her own impudence. She was staring about at the gathered Masters and mabinogs with open curiosity and, as it appeared to Rhydian, crass familiarity. Her glance lighted on one of the bards.

"Finian?" she said.

The new Master's eyes popped. "Y-yes, that's right. H-how did you —?"

"You don't know me, do you?" The young woman just smiled at him, then her gaze continued to sweep the room.

"Now listen here —" Master Rhydian began.

"Mistress Derwena!" she called out, once again interrupting the Storyteller. She strode through the gathered mabinogs and came before old Derwena, sitting in her Master's chair close to the hearth.

The Mistress's eyes had grown weak, and many suspected that there would be a new Master of Woodcraft before spring. Yet for the first time in months the Woodcrone stirred, and interest brought life into her quiet face.

The stranger knelt before her and took off her cloak, unfastening an ornate clasp fashioned as a rose to do so. Then she took the Woodcrone's gnarled hands in her own. "You know me, don't you, Mistress?" she asked.

A smile played about the old woman's mouth. "Are you mad, a broken soul, or a bard?" she asked.

"Bard, Mistress."

Derwena nodded. "I had thought it would be so, but the years have been long. I was losing hope, my child."

"No need for that. Not as long as the rose of the Eastern King still blooms," the stranger replied. Then she opened the purse at her belt, withdrawing a glorious red rose in full flower. The scent of it seemed to fill the room and drive the shadows away. She placed the bloom in the Mistress's hands. "I've brought you back the sprig," she said. "Or part of it, anyway."

The Master of Storytelling decided things had gone far enough. "Am I to understand, Mistress, that you know this person?" he asked in his most frosty tone.

The Mistress turned to him. "Know her? I knew her, as did you. As to what she has become, I'm sure we'll all know soon enough."

The Master frowned. "I do not believe I am acquainted with the young woman," he began again.

"Yes, Master Storyteller, you are." The stranger laughed and many were there who said afterwards that they heard the echo of fairy laughter in her voice. "It's me, Master. It's Meryl."

There was amazement among the Masters, and confusion among the mabinogs. Meryl, the runaway! Meryl, the banished one! Meryl ... there were many stories, told mostly by the mabinogs, of her fate.

The Master of Storytelling was staggered. "Ah, welcome home, child ..." His greeting faded away.

Meryl looked at the Mistress of Woodcraft and smiled. "Not home, Master. My quest continues, and it takes me far from here. But I would like to share your fire, and give you some new stories in return."

She sat down then, cross-legged on the floor, her back to the fire. There was a rumble of disapproval; this was not the way the Hall instructed bards to tell a story. From her pack she pulled a small harp. Nimbly she ran her fingers over its strings and began to tune the instrument, with the skill of long practice. Some of the Masters leaned forward. They saw what harp it was she held, and they each wished to call back this treasure for the Hall. But when she began to speak, they soon forgot all else.

"I have a story to tell," she said simply. Her voice rang out through the Hall. "It's the story of a rose and a King, and how they brought hope to our world."

And the bard began to sing her tale.

F.A. **DATE DUE**

FOLLETT

Pebble Bilingual Books

Soy respetuoso/
I Am Respectful

de/by
Sarah L. Schuette

Traducción/Translation
Martín Luis Guzmán Ferrer, Ph.D.

Capstone Press
Mankato, Minnesota

Pebble Bilingual Books are published by Capstone Press
151 Good Counsel Drive, P.O. Box 669, Mankato, Minnesota 56002
http://www.capstone-press.com

1 2 3 4 5 6 08 07 06 05 04 03

Library of Congress Cataloging-in-Publication Data
Schuette, Sarah L., 1976–
   [I am respectful. Spanish & English]
   Soy respetuoso / de Sarah L. Schuette; traducción, Martín Luis Guzmán Ferrer =
I am respectful / by Sarah L. Schuette; translation, Martín Luis Guzmán Ferrer.
   p. cm.—(Pebble bilingual books)
   Spanish and English.
   Includes index.
   Summary: Simple text and photographs show various ways children can be
respectful.
   ISBN 0-7368-2305-0
   1. Respect—Juvenile literature. [1. Respect. 2. Spanish language materials—
Bilingual.] I. Title: I am respectful. II. Title. III. Series: Pebble bilingual books.
BJ1533.R4S3818 2004
179'.9—dc21   2003004952

Credits
Mari C. Schuh and Martha E. H. Rustad, editors; Jennifer Schonborn, book designer
   and illustrator; Patrick Dentinger, cover production designer; Gary Sundermeyer,
   photographer; Nancy White, photo stylist; Karen Risch, product planning editor;
   Eida Del Risco, Spanish copy editor; Gail Saunders-Smith, consulting editor;
   Madonna Murphy, Ph.D., Professor of Education, University of St. Francis, Joliet,
   Illinois, author of *Character Education in America's Blue Ribbon Schools*, consultant

Pebble Books thanks the North Mankato Taylor Library in North Mankato,
Minnesota, and the Distad family of Mankato, Minnesota, for assistance with photo
shoots.

Table of Contents

Contenido

I am respectful. I treat
people the way I want
to be treated.

Yo soy respetuoso. Trato
a las personas como
quiero que ellas
me traten a mí.

I respect myself. I take care of myself.

Me respeto a mí mismo. Me cuido.

8

I respect the earth.

I recycle newspapers.

Respeto la Tierra.

Reciclo los periódicos.

I show respect to other
people. I shake hands
with the people I meet.

Muestro respeto por los
demás. Le doy la mano
a las personas cuando
me las presentan.

RESTROOMS

♿ MEN

12

I show respect by waiting patiently for my turn.

Muestro respeto esperando pacientemente mi turno.

I whisper when I am in the library.

Hablo quedito cuando estoy en la biblioteca.

Library Book Return

16

I am careful with
things that belong
to other people.

Soy cuidadoso con
las cosas que pertenecen
a los demás.

I thank people
who help me.

Doy las gracias
a las personas
cuando me ayudan.

I am respectful and kind.
I think about the feelings
of other people.

Soy respetuoso y
bondadoso. Pienso en los
sentimientos de los demás.

Glossary

feeling—an emotion such as happiness or sadness; people who are respectful care about the feelings of other people.

kind—friendly, helpful, and generous

recycle—to use old items so that they can be used again in new products

respect—to believe in the quality and worth of others and yourself; people who are respectful treat others the way they would like to be treated.

thank—to tell someone that you are grateful

treat—to act toward people in a certain way; respectful people treat others with kindness.

whisper—to talk very quietly or softly

Glosario

sentimiento *(el)*—emoción como la felicidad o la tristeza; a las personas respetuosas les importan los sentimientos de los demás.

bondadoso—ser afectuoso, útil y generoso

reciclar—emplear cosas usadas de tal manera que puedan aprovecharse en productos nuevos

respetar—creer en el valor y la calidad de los demás y de uno mismo; las personas respetuosas tratan a los demás como quieren que ellas las traten.

dar gracias—decirle a alguien que uno está agradecido

tratar—actuar con las personas de cierta manera; las personas respetuosas tratan a los demás bondadosamente.

hablar quedito—hablar en voz baja y suavemente

Index

Índice